"With humor and a wealth of knowledge to impart about folk pottery, Stanley creates an interesting plot and an amiable protagonist, and this novel could be the first in a notable collection."   —*Richmond Times-Dispatch*

"Stanley writes a fabulous who-done-it."
                    —*Midwest Book Review*

"An outstanding prize . . . J. B. Stanley also knows how to write, and write well, in the murder mystery vein. With her first book in this series, Ms. Stanley has written what few novice authors in this genre accomplish; and that is a very good mystery story with all the accoutrements of a seasoned pro."   —*Who Dunnit*

"A very likable amateur sleuth . . . I'll be happy to follow Molly on her future investigations."
                    —*The Romance Readers Connection*

"An entertaining, pleasant read."   —*Fresh Fiction*

"Stanley writes a good mystery as well as giving the reader a lesson in pottery making."   —*Roundtable Reviews*

Berkley Prime Crime Titles by J. B. Stanley

A KILLER COLLECTION
A FATAL APPRAISAL
A DEADLY DEALER

A Deadly Dealer

J. B. STANLEY

BERKLEY PRIME CRIME, NEW YORK

THE BERKLEY PUBLISHING GROUP
Published by the Penguin Group
Penguin Group (USA) Inc.
375 Hudson Street, New York, New York 10014, USA
Penguin Group (Canada), 90 Eglinton Avenue East, Suite 700, Toronto, Ontario M4P 2Y3, Canada
(a division of Pearson Penguin Canada Inc.)
Penguin Books Ltd., 80 Strand, London WC2R 0RL, England
Penguin Group Ireland, 25 St. Stephen's Green, Dublin 2, Ireland (a division of Penguin Books Ltd.)
Penguin Group (Australia), 250 Camberwell Road, Camberwell, Victoria 3124, Australia
(a division of Pearson Australia Group Pty. Ltd.)
Penguin Books India Pvt. Ltd., 11 Community Centre, Panchsheel Park, New Delhi—110 017, India
Penguin Group (NZ), 67 Apollo Drive, Rosedale, North Shore 0745, Auckland, New Zealand
(a division of Pearson New Zealand Ltd.)
Penguin Books (South Africa) (Pty.) Ltd., 24 Sturdee Avenue, Rosebank, Johannesburg 2196, South
Africa

Penguin Books Ltd., Registered Offices: 80 Strand, London WC2R 0RL, England

This is a work of fiction. Names, characters, places, and incidents either are the product of the author's imagination or are used fictitiously, and any resemblance to actual persons, living or dead, business establishments, events, or locales is entirely coincidental. The publisher does not have any control over and does not assume any responsibility for author or third-party websites or their content.

A DEADLY DEALER

A Berkley Prime Crime Book / published by arrangement with the author

PRINTING HISTORY
Berkley Prime Crime mass-market edition / August 2007

Copyright © 2007 by Jennifer Stanley.
Cover art by Mary Ann Lasher.
Cover design by Erica Tricarico.
Interior text design by Kristin del Rosario.

ISBN: 978-0-425-21670-5

BERKLEY® PRIME CRIME
Berkley Prime Crime Books are published by The Berkley Publishing Group,
a division of Penguin Group (USA) Inc.,
375 Hudson Street, New York, New York 10014.
The name BERKLEY PRIME CRIME and the BERKLEY PRIME CRIME design are trademarks belonging to Penguin Group (USA) Inc.

PRINTED IN THE UNITED STATES OF AMERICA

10 9 8 7 6 5 4 3 2 1

For my husband, Tim, with love
I'm your biggest fan

"There is a group of walking sticks called gadget canes . . . They have existed from time immemorial, ever since man has tried to conceal something in his stick to give him an advantage over an unsuspecting fellow man (weapon cane), or to smuggle something in or out of the country, or to ease the carrying of more than one item at the same time (tradesmen's cane)."

Francis H. Monek, *Canes Through the Ages*

A VILLAGE WEST OF DUSSELDORF, PRUSSIA, 1805

Heinrich listened in rapt attention as the village's new minister spoke the words of the Scripture. The man had astounded them when he had arrived just after dawn, walking up the dirt track and calling for all to wake and attend a sunrise worship service. The stranger's commanding voice had stirred the groggy into wakefulness, and the rhythmic clanging of the hand bell he carried easily echoed throughout the whole of the tiny village.

Once a crowd had gathered outside the church, the stranger introduced himself as Pastor Francke and solemnly announced that he had been sent as a replacement for the recently deceased Pastor Klein. Their former minister, who had fallen gravely ill a fortnight prior and had never regained consciousness, had been a kind and gentle soul with a skill for healing. It had been weeks since the peasants had attended a worship service and few noted the difference in routine; they were poor farmers and simple tradesmen whose main concern was the endless whining of their hungry bellies. However, unlearned as they were, the villagers recognized a figure of authority when they saw one and mumbled nervously to one another as they took their seats inside the church.

Unlike their previous spiritual leader, Pastor Francke was young and sturdy and spoke with a firmness that unnerved most of the villagers. After his parishioners had all warily settled into seats, he demanded silence and then declared his intention to bring his wayward flock closer to God's grace through toil, sacrifice, and long hours of prayer.

The only person out of the congregation who seemed satisfied by the new minister was Heinrich the Smith. He was pleased to listen to a youthful voice filled with such boldness and strength. Heinrich agreed that his fellow villagers needed to be taught a few lessons in obedience and felt that he had found a brother in Pastor Francke, as Heinrich was an angry man with a propensity for bullying the weak. He savored the biblical passages about revenge or bloodshed as a child relishes a fresh honey cake. Heinrich fixed his gaze upon the flickering candles on the altar and listened as Pastor Francke stared down from the pulpit and practically shouted at the villagers.

"The LORD said to Moses and Aaron, When Pharaoh says to you, 'Perform a miracle,' then say to Aaron, 'Take your staff and throw it down before Pharaoh, and it will become a snake.' So Moses and Aaron went to Pharaoh and did just as the LORD commanded. Aaron threw his staff down in front of Pharaoh and his officials, and it became a snake. Pharaoh then summoned wise men and sorcerers, and the Egyptian magicians also did the same things by their secret arts: Each one threw down his staff and it became a snake. But Aaron's staff swallowed up their staffs. Yet Pharaoh's heart became hard and he would not listen to them, just as the LORD had said."

Heinrich looked over at his wife, Gerta, but she was sitting demurely with her eyes cast downward, focusing in-

tently on the lap of her brown homespun skirt. Heinrich felt his ire rising. He clenched his fists into tight, bloodless knots. Gerta was deliberately avoiding the lustful looks of her lover, Jacob the Miller, who sat across the aisle from them. Heinrich was no fool. He had seen the couple steal off into the woods together early yester morn. Gerta carried a pile of clothes to wash against the rocks, but Jacob had followed her empty-handed, without even bothering to pretend that he had some genuine errand at the stream.

Heinrich had hobbled after them, his Hazelwood cane supporting the weight of his twisted right leg. When he was a boy, Heinrich had been trampled by a horse as his father tried to shoe the frightened beast. After many weeks in bed, Heinrich was finally able to stand, but he could not walk without a crutch. One day, his father took him into the forest and showed him how to cut a long branch from the Hazelwood tree. They cut the limb below the trunk and down into the dirt so that the gnarled and fistlike root clump was still attached. After boiling the wood for an entire day, the bark came off in feathery strips and Heinrich was given a small knife with which to carve out a handle from the root clump.

Throughout the winter he perfected the artistry of his first cane, delighted to discover that he was a natural woodworker. He carved an incredibly realistic horse head out of the root ball, boring holes for the eyes, which he later filled with two matched, white pebbles from the streambed. The white eyes made the horse look crazed. One half-expected froth to bubble from between the beast's wooden lips. Lastly, after Heinrich had sanded the shaft with fish skin until it was as smooth as rabbit fur and gleamed with inner life in the firelight, he began to use it on the other boys in the village.

It was with this cane that Heinrich learned how to command respect. If the boys called him a cripple, he lay in wait for them behind a tree in the forest or one of the village's crude huts and then lashed at them repeatedly with his cane. His prey could only hope to escape Heinrich's wrath by running away, but Heinrich never forgot a slight and was infinitely patient when it came to seeking revenge. Soon, the village children learned not to taunt him. He became a loner, but this suited him. At night, after working for his father, he would polish his horse-head cane and whisper to it intimately until even his parents were spooked by their own progeny.

As a man, Heinrich continued to make canes. When Napoleon's armies invaded the Rhineland and threatened to burn Heinrich's smithy along with the rest of the town's structures, he quickly offered the officer in charge a splendid cane with a dagger hidden within its shaft and a proud hunting hound carved into the handle. The Frenchman, who had an entire pack of hounds back on his estate, was immediately stricken with homesickness and not only spared Heinrich's hut in exchange for the gift, but allowed the entire village to remain unsullied by his soldiers.

Begrudgingly, the villagers proclaimed Heinrich a hero and he continued to sell canes, swords, and horseshoes to the French battalions as they traveled through the village toward Hamburg. Heinrich grew prosperous during the French occupation, but his wife became more and more disgusted with every coin he earned.

"How can you deal with those French dogs?" she hissed one night as she sat on a low stool in front of the fire, her moss-colored eyes sparkling with angry disgust. "Better to let them burn our homes to the ground then take their coin. If I had any sons, I would raise them to fight instead of to kiss the enemy's hairy arses as their father does."

Heinrich stood and, quick as lightning, slapped his wife's fair cheek. A crimson handprint bloomed upon her face but she barely flinched beneath his blow. She stared at him with an intense hatred before wordlessly resuming her mending. Gerta's outspokenness and inability to conceive vexed him greatly, and his wife made no attempt to hide her belief that Heinrich was at fault—a cripple in more than one way.

But since he had spied on Gerta and Jacob coupling in the woods, Heinrich's sense of impotent manhood had been transformed into a seething, quiet rage. He would not be humiliated by her brazenness and her wanton ways as well. Gerta needed to be taught a lesson.

The words of the Scripture brought Heinrich's thoughts back to the moment. Even after the congregation filed out of the small chapel, a particular phrase resonated within the chambers of Heinrich's black heart: ". . . stretch out your hand over the waters of Egypt—over the streams and canals, over the ponds and all the reservoirs—and they will turn to blood. Blood will be everywhere in Egypt, even in the wooden buckets and stone jars."

The worship service had ended but Heinrich still sat visualizing a river of blood as it surged down the dirt road of his own village. As he thought about blood, an idea began to form in Heinrich's mind. He shuffled forward to where Pastor Francke was sharing some herblore with a pregnant villager. Seeing the swollen belly on the woman who had not yet been married a year incensed Heinrich further, and when she moved away, he hastily spoke up before Pastor Francke could leave to settle into the home allotted to him and break his morning's fast.

"Pastor?" he began gruffly, unaccustomed to addressing another with respect.

"Yes?"

"Do you think God believes that His followers are allowed to hand out vengeance when they are certain someone has committed a sin?"

Pastor Francke studied Heinrich cautiously, taking in his crooked leg and the zealous gleam in his parishioner's black eyes. He sensed that his answer should be carefully guarded and that Heinrich was like a headstrong and rebellious child who needed to be quickly brought under thumb.

"Why do you ask? Do you know someone who has committed such a grave sin?" he asked warily, keeping his tone flat.

Heinrich had a feeling that despite his volatile preaching, Pastor Francke might not be the accomplice he had hoped for. "Ah . . . no, Father." He shook his head dumbly. "It is just that I cannot read but I would like to see for myself what the word looks like."

Perplexed, the minister asked, "Vengeance?"

Heinrich nodded in assent.

It was a singularly odd request, but Pastor Francke was proud of his learning and eager to show off his skills, even if it was only to the benefit of an ignorant peasant.

"Come outside. I shall show you."

Heinrich followed the pastor to a patch of dirt next to the church. The pastor retrieved a stick and began to scratch letters into the soil. Heinrich could write his own name, but did not recognize all of the letters etched into the dust. He was fortunate, however, in that he could remember any symbol once he had seen it written out before him. Thus, he committed to memory every stroke made by the pastor's skeletal stick.

"That is the word?" Heinrich asked eagerly.

Tossing the stick aside, Pastor Francke nodded. "Yes. That is how you write vengeance. I am curious as to why you are so interested in that particular word. Perhaps you could join me for a personal prayer session in order to enlighten me?" He brushed some dust from the hem of his dark robe. "But not now. I shall be quite busy for the remainder of the day. I will send for you when I am ready."

"Thank you, Pastor. Good day to you," Heinrich said, limping away hurriedly.

"What is your rush, husband?" his wife called after

him. When he failed to respond, she turned back to the bevy of women gossiping outside the church. The sound of her laughter mocked his uneven gait as he headed for the woods.

Stopping by his smithy to collect an axe, Heinrich journeyed deep into the forest. He sought an ash tree blackened by a tongue of lightning many years ago. It had flourished despite its wound and Heinrich wished to capture its strength. As he approached the tree, he raised his sharpened axe blade into the air. "I shall take the very heart from you and you will die," Heinrich addressed the tree with a reverence he felt for few living things. "But with your wood I will make my finest cane. This cane I shall call Die Rache *(Vengeance)*."

Chapter 1

"Then, of course, there is the typical German walking stick, which is purchased on vacation, decorated with cane nails and brought home as a souvenir. Its decoration, vanity and actual uselessness is what makes the walking stick a strolling stick."

ULRICH KLEVER, WALKINGSTICKS

"**R**idiculous!" snorted Clara Appleby in disgust as she roughly smoothed a miniscule wrinkle in her paprika-colored cardigan. "Look at that woman!" She turned to her daughter, Molly, who was lost in the charms of yet another Agatha Christie novel. She had been reading the Hercule Poirot novels all summer long, but had yet to figure out which character was the killer until the eccentric little Belgian announced his findings. Jabbing at her daughter's flank with a sharp elbow, Clara was pleased to see a pair of gray eyes framed with long, curling black lashes look up at her in irritation.

"Ma! Hercule was just about to announce the murderer," Molly complained. "And I'm positive I know who it is this time. What are you grumping about, anyway? We haven't even left the tarmac yet."

"That," said Clara, pointing down the narrow airplane aisle at a mammoth woman coming toward them, wearing a chartreuse sack dress. Two yellow-and-tangerine-spotted giraffes were embroidered on the dress pockets and a wooden giraffe pendant dangled from a chunky bead necklace circumnavigating the woman's nonexistent neck. Fluorescent orange lipstick matched a set of acrylic nails, which flapped about like zealous monarch butterflies. The woman dragged a bulbous carry-on suitcase behind her as she babbled animatedly into her cell phone.

"Why don't they force people to check bags of that size?" Clara demanded. "You could fit a small child in there. Ugh. We'll *never* leave on time at this rate."

Molly tucked her book into the seat pocket in front of her and sat back in order to observe the source of her mother's distress with amusement. As a reporter for *Collector's Weekly,* frequent trips were a necessity for Molly and she was all too familiar with the trials of modern travel. Of course, most of her excursions were taken by car, but she noticed that a motorist's bad manners, whether it be tailgating or talking on a cell phone while veering across three lanes of traffic with no turn signal, were shortcomings that easily translated to aerial travel. Molly sighed, noting the long, stagnant line of passengers held up by Giraffe Lady as she searched for an overhead compartment large enough to hold her gargantuan carry-on. Spotting a bin, she transferred her phone to another ear and made a feeble attempt at lifting her bag. After uttering an impish "Oh!" it was clear that she did not possess enough strength to even raise it an inch off the ground.

Glancing around helplessly, her riotous chatter uninterrupted by her predicament, the woman's eyes fell upon a young businessman reading the newspaper. Sensing that he was being watched, the man looked up, took a quick glance at the line of aggravated travelers clotting the aisle, and leaped from his seat to assist. In one flourish, he hauled the bag into the air and into the compartment, where it stuck firmly halfway in and halfway out of the space. He gave it a gentle shove, turned it on its axis, and finally began to force the carry-on roughly into the overhead using his shoulders as leverage.

"Be careful! My makeup's in there!" the woman squealed in a high-pitched voice, and then began to complain vociferously to her caller that airplanes did not provide adequate service when it came to assisting the handicapped.

Clara raked her eyes up and down the woman's physique and muttered, "Handicapped? Her only handicap is that her phone seems to have been surgically implanted onto her ear." Molly laughed heartily as the suitcase was finally wedged into the bin and the businessman collapsed into his seat with relief.

The woman mouthed a neon orange, "Oh, thank you, dear," to the perspiring young man and waddled beyond the row where the Appleby women sat, who both shot daggers in her direction. Of course she was unaware of their hostile stares as her attention was entirely focused on her interminable phone conversation.

"We *are* going to be late taking off," Molly griped, checking her watch. Their plane was scheduled to leave the gate in five minutes.

"Well, we'll still be there in plenty of time for the preview party," Clara assured her, opening an auction catalogue featuring folk and outsider art.

"I can't wait to get to Nashville," Molly said, perking up. "I've always wanted to stay at the Opryland Hotel."

"It's an awesome place. That is, *if* we ever get there. Look, here's another character holding us up."

A squat man with a ruddy complexion barreled down the aisle, knocking into all of the seated passengers with either his laptop case, which was slung over his shoulder, or the trench coat folded over his other arm. Every few rows he had to stop and apologize to another mildly wounded passenger.

"Ow, watch it!" complained an elderly lady who sustained a harsh blow to the shoulder from the leather computer satchel. "This is why I hate the aisle!" she complained pointedly to her husband. "You always get the window or the middle seat and *I* get accosted by nincompoops and drink carts."

"Sorry, so sorry," the red-faced man apologized, smiling and coming to an abrupt halt next to the old lady. "This laptop gets filled with more and more data from Monday to Friday. It just keeps getting heavier and heavier!" he bellowed as he looked around to see if he had an audience. He then patted his rotund paunch expansively. "Guess it's just trying to keep up with me! Ha, ha!" His grating guffaw reverberated inside the stuffy cabin.

One or two other passengers offered polite grins in response to his self-deprecating joke, but Molly groaned.

"Oh no, this guy is a major talker. He's going to be in the seat next to me, I just know it. How did I get stuck in the middle, anyway?" she asked her mother accusingly.

Clara gave an innocent shrug of her shoulders. "You know I need to stretch my left leg into the aisle. Ever since that knee surgery, I've been stiff as your grandmother's fruitcake. Uh-oh, I think you were right. Mr. Big Shot is eyeing our row."

"Ladies!" The boisterous man greeted them in a horrendous attempt at a gallant English accent. "I *do* believe I shall be joining you!" And without waiting for either woman to stand, he began pushing himself forward into their row. Clara grabbed a commanding hold of his arm and dug her long fingers into his flesh. "You can just wait until we get out," she admonished him.

Halfway into the row he swung around so quickly to look at Clara, that his laptop case arced into the air and smacked into Molly's cheek with a loud *thwap*. Pressing a palm against her smarting skin, Molly stepped aside and cast her mother a woeful look as their new neighbor thrust his bulk forward to the window seat. "Save me," she whispered mournfully to Clara.

Once everyone was finally seated, Molly immediately opened her book and pretended to be completely absorbed, though it was difficult to concentrate on Poirot's sleuthing when her row mate was shifting about so dramatically in his seat. In fact, the entire left side of his body had invaded Molly's space. As a result, she drifted into her mother's space.

"Now where *is* that seat belt?" the man laughed. "Those rascally things are always hiding from me. You don't have it, do you?" he asked flirtatiously.

Molly wordlessly pointed to where the belt hung from the side of his seat. He laughed again. As if it had been waiting for him to be safely belted in, the plane gave a sudden lurch and began to pull back from the gate. Molly, finally feeling that they might actually make it to Nashville somewhat on schedule, once again opened her book, but her neighbor roughly jammed her shoulder while digging around in his back pocket for something. Molly caught a whiff of beer breath. Pressing her body farther against her mother, who was giggling in silent mirth, Molly whispered, "I am taking the aisle on the way home, I'll have you know."

Once the plane had reached cruising altitude, Molly's neighbor cleared his throat and prepared to ruin the hour of bliss in which she had planned to keep her nose rooted in her book.

"Do you live in Nashville?" he asked, reclining his seat back until it practically rested on the knees of the tall man seated behind him.

"No, just visiting," Molly answered tersely without looking up.

"Nice time of year for vacation. There some country music concert or something you're seeing?" he persisted.

"An antique show, actually," Molly replied, rereading the same sentence for the third time. She braced herself for his next question.

"Antiques, hey?" He chuckled. "You're flying out to

Nashville just for an antique show. Must be mighty special."

Molly sighed and closed her book. "Actually, I'm a reporter. I'm covering the show for my paper, *Collector's Weekly*."

"Ah, a *working* vacation!" He puffed out his chest importantly. "Now, *that's* something I can relate to 'cause *that's* what *I'm* doing. Going to a convention at the Opryland Hotel. I'm an insurance man. Do you have life insurance, young lady?"

Clara's shoulders jiggled again as she laughed noiselessly. Molly dug her elbow into her mother's ribs. "Yes, lots," she quickly lied. "My job has great benefits."

"Hope so," the man answered gravely. "My name's Al. Short name, long on character."

"Nice to meet you." Molly cast him a polite grin and then averted her eyes.

Undeterred, Al launched into a monologue about the cities he had recently visited, the awards he had won over the course of his career, and his list of best and worst barbeque restaurants east of the Mississippi.

"That your older sister next to you?" Al asked during a brief pause in which Molly dared to reopen her book. He winked dramatically in Clara's direction. "I think I can spot a family resemblance."

Molly groaned inwardly and looked over at her mother. Everywhere they went together people always said that. Of course it was a compliment for her mother, but how old did they think Molly was if her mother looked like her sister?

Thirty years old, that's how I look, Molly thought glumly. Yet, if she aged as well as her mother had, she could count herself lucky. Clara sat in an upright, imperial posture, flicking purposefully through *Sky Mall*, the airplane's catalogue of superfluous luxury merchandise. She had a thick crown of dark hair styled into an angled bob, an aquiline nose, and an expressive mouth that often displayed signs of impatience. Her intelligent eyes gazed upon the world with confidence. At fifty-five, Clara was a regally tall and trim woman radiating good health. She still managed to capture the stares of men of all ages.

Molly had inherited Clara's facial features, but she wore her chocolate-colored hair long and straight; it fell in a shiny cascade to her shoulders. She was tall as well, but slightly shorter than Clara and much, much rounder. A size fourteen, Molly had a deep love of sweets and rarely denied herself a daily treat. With a full bosom, a fairly narrow waist, and wide hips, Molly had all the curves of Marilyn Monroe back when she was brunette Norma Jean.

"That's my *mother*," Molly replied huffily and then looked up in relief as the flight attendant neared their row. She was more than ready to embrace any sort of distraction.

"I don't see her handing out any food," Clara grumbled.

"You don't get food on planes anymore, Ma. That's why I packed us turkey sandwiches."

Clara grunted. "For the price of tickets these days, we should all be getting filet mignon."

Al shouted, "Here, here!" and was still roaring with raucous laughter when the flight attendant handed them each a bag of pretzels, her overly-tweezed eyebrows arched in curiosity.

"Anything to drink?" she mechanically asked Al while deftly reaching across Molly and Clara with a cocktail napkin.

"Got any beer to go with this bit of starch, darlin'?" he inquired eagerly.

A flicker of disapproval appeared in the flight attendant's eyes. "I'm not sure. On a flight this short . . ." Her insinuation was lost on Al. "I'll check. Ladies? What can I get for you?"

Clara requested a bottled water for herself and a Diet Coke for Molly. She then counted out the eight minuscule pretzels in her bag, Molly unrolled the turkey sandwiches and took a grateful bite, hoping to resume her reading while Al crunched noisily on his pretzels.

"These would go much better with the King of Beers," he said to no one in particular. Molly ignored him and, for the fourth time, read the sentence she had begun reading before Al sat down. Hercule Poirot was standing in front of a mirror and once again relishing the splendor of his moustache when Al tapped Molly on the shoulder.

"Do you see that stewardess anywhere? I think she forgot about me."

"Hit the call button on your seat," Molly suggested, pitying the flight attendant but willing to sacrifice the woman in favor of Agatha Christie.

At that moment, the captain announced their initial descent into Nashville and the flight attendant came back up the aisle to check for reclined seats, unfastened safety belts, or tray tables that were not in their full upright and locked position. Al was in violation of all three and the flight attendant admonished him in a cold, yet carefully gracious manner.

"I never did get my beer," he mumbled petulantly to her retreating figure and then fell silent for the first time since takeoff.

"I'm sure they have a bar at the hotel," Molly said, feeling charitable as Nashville's airport came into view below a layer of sporadic clouds.

Al brightened at the thought. "They have a *whole* bunch of bars. One of 'em even turns in a circle while you're sitting there. A few too many brewskis and you might just fall off the side into the waterfall."

"Your hotel has a waterfall?" Molly asked in surprise, thinking that Al must have been taking nips from a flask hidden in the depths of his trench coat.

"Oh, they've got a whole river in that place. You can really get lost there. Gaylord Opryland is famous all over the world!" Al exclaimed proudly, as if he had built the five-star hotel with his own bare hands. "Where are you two staying, by the way?"

"Just some chain hotel," Molly fibbed hastily, fearing that Al would want to meet for drinks if he learned they were both staying at the same place.

"Too bad." Al clucked his tongue. "You're really missing out. Me and a few of my buddies really know how to close down a bar. Hey, you single?" he inquired slyly.

"Spoken for," Molly answered happily and gazed into the rippled clouds beyond Al's head. She allowed herself to reminisce once again about the candlelit anniversary dinner she had just celebrated with coworker-turned-boyfriend, Mark Harrison. They had officially been dating for one glorious year. She touched the heart locket he had given her and tried for the hundredth time not to wish that it would magically transform into a sparkly engagement ring. Even back when she had opened the locket at the pricey restaurant Mark had taken her to, she had quietly prayed that it would contain a message inside, but instead, it held miniature portraits of her two cats, Merlin and Griffin. No tiny slip reading *"Will you marry me?"* came fluttering out, much to Molly's (and Clara's) great disappointment.

"No ring yet, though, I see," Al teased, honing in on Molly's last thought like a malicious psychic. "A pretty thing like you, and your man lets you run around the country by yourself?" He snorted. "He's sure a trusting fellow." He eyed Molly's chest. "Still, you're officially single. That means you can still go out and play. Here's my card," Al slipped a business card into the leaves of Molly's closed book. "Call my cell if you need any entertaining while you're in Nashville. After all, how exciting can an antique show be?"

And with that said, the plane thankfully landed with such an acute screeching of tires that Molly was thoroughly prevented from responding to Al's preposterous series of remarks.

Nothing could have prepared Molly for the sheer enormity of the Opryland Hotel. Its lobby was easily the length of half a football field, covered with lush carpets, and lit by dozens of glimmering chandeliers the size of dinner tables. As she and Clara maneuvered themselves around pods of tour groups, valets, bellhops, and what appeared to be a cluster of Dolly Parton lookalikes wearing sequined gowns and padded bras, Clara pointed euphorically to a gilded trolley beyond the reception desk.

"That, my dear, is the tea trolley. The world's finest piece of carrot cake awaits you after we check in."

Molly's stomach did an excited flip as she hustled herself in front of a family of six in order to enter the stanchion maze corralling guests waiting to check in. A large group of Japanese tourists were chattering animatedly in front of Molly. The men were dressed casually in polo shirts and jeans and carried red Japan Airlines vinyl flight bags. The women were decked out in designer suits of all colors and were accessorized with jewelry, scarves, and sunglasses fresh from the pages of *Vogue*. Molly, who only took note of the latest fashions during her regular visits to the nail salon, had never seen such a collection of Prada, Fendi, Gucci, Yves Saint Laurent, or Luis Vuitton in one room.

Shoving her Kate Spade knockoff purse farther back on her shoulder, she whispered to her mother, "Exactly how much is our room again?" She subtly gestured toward the group of Japanese women. "'Cause I think the contents of those women's suitcases are worth more than the entire inventory of my house."

"Nonsense." Clara waved dismissively. "You can always get your money out of antiques. Every item those women are wearing is depreciating in value as we stand here. Besides, we got a special rate for the Heart of Dixie show. Even your tight-fisted boss can't burst a blood vessel over this room. Ah . . . it's finally our turn."

"Welcome to Nashville," their desk clerk greeted them warmly. "Clara and Molly Appleby? Yes, we have you in a lovely garden room overlooking the waterfall. Here is a map to your room. See this symbol? That's the main lobby. Turn right here, go to this set of elevators, and proceed to the fourth floor. Your room will be down the hallway to the right. We suggest you keep this map with you when you move about the hotel. Enjoy your stay, ladies."

Molly clutched the map with some trepidation and followed her mother to the tea trolley. Moments later, she was sinking her teeth into the freshest, most fragrantly delectable piece of carrot cake in existence. Raisins popped with bursts of flavor in her cheek, soft strips of carrots blended with nutmeg and cinnamon on her tongue, and the two inches of buttercream frosting scooped into her mouth from her fork were so tantalizingly sweet that her teeth began to protest at the sugary onslaught.

"My dear lord!" she breathed and then took a deep sip of tea. "That should be outlawed."

"You'll be glad you ate that cake later on. There's never enough food at the preview party." Clara briskly dusted some powdered sugar that had fallen from the spongy surface of her raspberry lemon square off of her pant leg. "Now, let's go find our room. Got the map, Marco Polo?"

Molly successfully navigated them to the fourth floor and slid the key card into their door. As soon as it was opened, a burst of cigarette smoke wafted out of the room, as if being chased by a forceful breeze.

"Somehow I doubt this is a non-smoking room," Molly stated the obvious.

"Well, I *certainly* asked for one!" Clara grumbled, striding across the floral carpet and throwing open the balcony doors. Their balcony contained a charming cast-iron patio set just big enough for two. Molly stepped outside and marveled at the sight: The balcony overlooked a verdant paradise of tropical trees and plants, which seemed to be growing so prolifically that the restaurant and bar tables far below were mostly obscured by their robust foliage. The sounds of the cascading waterfall assailed their ears with more of a loud purr than an abrasive roar, and several small birds flittered about the metal rafters beneath the sunlit glass roof.

"That waterfall's got to be forty feet high!"

"That's nothing," Clara remarked flatly. "See that circular area down there with the tables and chairs?"

Molly nodded.

"That's where we're having our cocktails. The whole bar turns in a slow circle while you're sitting there!"

"So our plane buddy, Al, was right," Molly mused. "I could see him having trouble stepping off a moving platform after a few beers."

Clara shrugged. "One can always hope that those sort would simply fall over the side into the lake. Good riddance, too. I can't stand loud talkers."

"Oh, forget about him. I feel like we're in the Brazilian equivalent of Chaco cliff dwellings!" Molly exclaimed. "Or inside a greenhouse made by giants. This place is fantastic."

"Except for the smoke." Clara frowned. "Call the front desk and see if you can get us another room in this area, will you, my candied praline?"

Molly rolled her eyes at the latest of Clara's confectionary monikers. "You only call me a baked good when you want me to do something."

The front desk was profusely apologetic that their non-smoking room had been invaded by a mysterious group of smokers in the time elapsed since the previous guests had checked out. He offered them a similar room just down the hall and promised to send up a bellhop immediately with a fresh key card. After waiting outside their new premises for ten minutes, Clara began to storm up and down the hallway.

"Where is our key? I'm getting tired and cross and we need to get dressed!"

At that opportune moment, a bellhop with sun-bleached hair, tanned skin, and a dazzlingly white smile bounded down the hall with boyish exuberance. He smelled faintly of Coppertone and practically bowed when he saw the look of impatience on Clara's face.

"Sorry, ladies." He smiled again, causing a series of dimples to appear on both cheeks. "I had to help a group of Japanese guests and we had some language difficulties. Here are two drink vouchers for the Cascades Terrace Lounge to make up for your inconvenience. And if there's anything you need," he eyed Molly suggestively, "*anything at all*, just ring for me." He tapped on his gold name badge. "I'm Wiley."

"I bet you are," Molly mumbled under her breath as her mother accepted the drink vouchers, all previous feelings of irritation clearly dispelled.

"Now, *that's* service!" Clara pronounced gaily as they entered their new room.

"To what are you referring, Ma, the drinks or the bellhop?"

"The drinks, of course. Now, let's get ready. I'm about ready for my free nip."

Molly tugged at the constrictive neck of her wool sweater for the third time and cast a surreptitiously envious glance at her mother's black sheath dress. Clara looked classy and comfortable in her washable linen, which she had dressed up with vintage accessories including a choker and matching bracelet of Victorian jet.

"Why did you pack that sweater?" Clara demanded, taking immediate notice of Molly's discomfort. "It's broiling in Nashville in October." She leaned over the glossy surface of their table and examined her daughter's neck. "You know you're allergic to 100 percent wool. I think I see hives blooming on your skin this very minute!"

"It's a blend, Ma," Molly scowled, refusing to admit that she was suffocating with both heat and prickly itchiness beneath the pumpkin-colored lambswool. "I just thought it was the perfect color to wear to the preview party."

"Go upstairs and put on something else," Clara ordered. "I'll get our drinks. Go on, it will only take you a second."

When Molly returned to the revolving bar, wearing a silk sweater set and a necklace made of miniature pieces of southern pottery, she noticed that their table had moved slightly west of the waterfall. Clara nodded in approval at Molly's second choice of attire and pushed a bowl of cocktail peanuts in her direction.

"By the end of the hour," Molly said cheerfully after taking a slurp of her cocktail, an iced creamy concoction called Nuts and Berries, "we'll have turned 180 degrees."

"My, my." Clara sank back into her chair. "Isn't this place wonderful? The sound of running water, tropical plants, and a double shot of Crown Royal and water that *actually* has two whole shots in it." She raised her glass to the bartender in salute. He bowed gallantly in return.

"Let me taste that," Molly requested.

"I don't see why, you won't like it," Clara retorted, but handed her daughter the thick tumbler.

Molly took a miniscule sip and coughed. "Ugh! How can you enjoy that? There are products for refinishing furniture that have less turpentine in them."

"Beware to whom you belittle fine whiskey, my dear. Besides, your grandfather always told me that if I was going to drink, I might as well drink the best. Crown Royal is a superior intoxicant."

"I guess it's an acquired taste," Molly conceded.

"Actually, I used to drink the same kind of sweet spirits that you do, dear. There will come a day when you will outgrow drinks accompanied by umbrellas or maraschino cherries."

"When did you grow out of them?"

Clara shrugged. "Honestly, the day you came home from the hospital."

Molly signaled for the waiter. Her mother so rarely talked about the days of Molly's infancy that she wanted to keep the words flowing.

"Well, in those times, hospitals were sensible. They knew that giving birth was a traumatic event. First of all, they knocked you out completely, which is a truly marvelous idea. Why *anyone* would want to be awake for the actual labor process is truly incomprehensible. Once you finally did deliver—your baby having been plucked neatly from your womb with a handy pair of forceps—you got an entire week in the hospital to rest and regain some sense of well-being and calm."

The waiter arrived with their second round and noiselessly scooped up their empty glasses. Molly absently chewed on her drink stirrer and willed her mother to continue. Clara's second whiskey seemed to help in the loosening of her tongue.

"I assumed that you'd be just as easy to manage at home as you had been in the hospital," she continued. "The nurses showed me how to change a diaper, feed you, and assured me that you'd sleep most of the time."

Molly sat up straighter. "So my father was there, too?"

Clara's eyes grew cloudy. "Oh sure, he made it through the first week of your life. In fact, he made it through exactly eight days. The day we brought you home proved to be his last."

"Why?" Molly asked in anguish. "Was I *that* bad?"

"Oh no, cupcake. You just turned as yellow as a lemon and wouldn't eat a thing. It was a little scary."

"So I had jaundice and . . . were you breast-feeding me?"

"I should say not!" Clara exclaimed in horror. "Thank goodness breast-feeding was not in vogue as it is now. No, no, you were a formula baby from the first. You ate beautifully in the hospital, you just wouldn't eat at home."

"What did you do?"

"I called the nurse who had taken care of me all week. She came over after her shift and told me to make sure you got some sunlight and brought me one of the bottles the hospital used. You drank up everything she fed you. See how stubborn you were, right from the get-go?"

"And what did Dad do?" Molly asked quietly, knowing that her mother might cease her narrative at any moment. Mentioning the man she had been married to for less than a year was a subject everyone knew to avoid with Clara Appleby. She had made it clear to all that the name of Nathan Appleby and anything relating to him was strictly taboo.

"Your *father* freaked out, that's what he did!" Clara practically shouted, her eyes flashing with anger. "Said we had decided never to have children and that he realized he couldn't handle being a father. Off he went into the sunset on that old Harley of his, and I had my first taste of bourbon. We could only afford the cheap stuff, but it was hardly a margarita moment, you see, so I drank it. And then I drank some more."

Molly was quiet. "Oh, Ma. I know you said he left, but I didn't think I was *that* young. No wonder I have no memory of him."

"You're better off this way, trust me." Clara took a deep swallow of her drink.

Suddenly the waiter appeared with another round. Clara eyed her daughter suspiciously. "You know I never have more than two, Molly."

"Don't look at me." Molly threw up her palms in a gesture of innocence.

"Ah, ma'am?" The waiter graciously interceded. "Compliments of the gentleman seated next to the bird-of-paradise."

Molly swiveled around in her chair in order to catch a glimpse of their benefactor. Seated at another bar table was a man with a lined and distinguished face, a carefully manicured silver beard and moustache, and an impeccable gray suit paired with a pink-and-white-striped tie. His eyes twinkled merrily as he issued an appreciative dip of the head, clearly meant for Clara.

Molly provided the gentleman with a quick smile and then turned her body back around as quickly as possible in order to catch her mother's reaction. Clara thanked her admirer with a regal nod and a close-lipped smile, her eyes alight with curiosity and something else that Molly had never seen before. Could her mother actually be attracted to a man? Molly had known many men to pursue her mother, for Clara was intelligent, cultured, ambitious, and stunningly attractive. And although Clara had deigned to share a meal or two with prospective suitors, no one had captured her interest long enough for any serious relationship to ever take root.

"These men all want me to take care of them," she had snorted a few months ago when Molly suggested that Clara might want to remarry one day. "Who needs that? Plus, the only wedding I want to be involved with is yours. Now that you're thirty, I would have thought you'd be a bit more aggressive about tying down that boyfriend of yours."

Molly brought her thoughts back to the present. "Do you know that man?" she asked her mother with avid interest.

"I know *who* he is. Everyone does," her mother whispered excitedly. "That's Grayson Montgomery."

"Of Montgomery Antiques & Rare Books? Out of Atlanta, Charleston, and Richmond?"

Clara nodded, trying not to steal a glance over at the famed antique dealer. "The same."

Molly was impressed. "Wow. I've never even seen a photo of him. He cuts quite a dashing figure. Have you ever met him before?"

"Oh." Clara put on an expression of nonchalance. "Twice before at this show, when I still had my own shop and was on the show circuit and once at a lecture in Charleston. He hasn't been to a show in years. He's got *people* to represent him at all of these types of venues now. In fact, I wonder why he's here. He must be on a buying trip."

As Clara snuck a sly look at Grayson, a willowy red-head approached his table and placed her hands proprietarily on a pair of angular hips. The Appleby women watched with avid interest as Grayson rose and then graciously offered his arm for the younger woman to take. The pair stepped lightly off of the platform but not before Grayson cast a sincere smile in their direction. Clara beamed in return, but her attention was then drawn to the back of the auburn stranger by his side.

"Who's that?" Molly asked.

"Don't know." Clara shrugged. "She may work at his booth."

"I didn't get a look at her face at all." Molly was disappointed.

At that moment, the woman glanced back over her shoulder and shot a venomous glance in their direction. With a flounce of her gorgeous mane, she clung to Grayson's arm more firmly and hastened her stride across the nearest bridge, practically dragging him along.

"What a nasty little fox." Clara glared at the retreating figures. She returned her attention to her daughter and then blushed ever so slightly, an action completely out of character. "Stop looking at me like that. Yes, he is handsome. Yes, he is enormously rich. And yes, he has excellent taste in arts and antiques, but he also happens to be married.

And that, my dear, is not his wife. I met her once, years ago. He must have a bevy of mistresses as well."

"No wonder. He looks like a southern Sean Connery," Molly muttered, her hopes at playing cupid dashed.

"Come on, let's go. If we finish these drinks we won't even know what we're looking at during the preview."

"Maybe I'll be checking out Grayson Montgomery's left hand, to see whether that wedding ring is still there," Molly teased. "And while I'm at it, maybe I'll find out exactly who that redheaded minx is."

"Don't be ridiculous. We have serious work to do tonight. We have to make a mad dash for the meat—they always run out—and then we have to find you a painted wall shelf to display your miniature Rebecca pitchers on."

"Fine, fine. But don't forget, I have an article to write, too. I think my first interview will take place in . . ." She flipped hurriedly through her show catalogue. "Booth number fourteen. Montgomery Antiques & Rare Books."

Chapter 2

There were at least fifty people already waiting in line to be the first to enter the large room where the Heart of Dixie Antique Show was being held. Nervous laughter and scores of hands tightly clenching orange-hued preview party tickets did little to alleviate Clara's anxiety that they had lingered too long at the bar.

"At least they've only just started letting people in," Clara said, craning her neck over the backs of those in line in front of her. "There might still be a few tasteless chicken wings left by the time we get inside."

The entrance to the show was restricted to one set of doors, propped open by two dignified matrons in black who accepted the orange tickets with gentile smiles.

"Y'all make sure to vote for the best jack-o'-lantern, ya hear?" they reminded each new group of incoming revelers while handing out ballots.

"What are they talking about?" Molly asked her mother as she looked at her ballot.

Clara's eyes remained riveted on the buffet spread up ahead. The food was now close enough to smell but the bodies of those helping themselves to heaping plates still obscured the particulars of the menu. It seemed to Molly that the diners in front of her were dithering about as they picked their way through the choicest morsels.

"We're going to be stuck eating cubes of Cheddar cheese," Clara grumbled and then turned her attention to her daughter. "In answer to your question . . . being that this *is* the Pumpkin Patch Preview Party, the show producers host a contest each year to see which dealer carves the most creative pumpkin. The ticket holders—that would be us—each get to vote on one pumpkin, and the winning dealer gets a pretty handsome prize. Sometimes their room here is paid for, which is a nice bonus when you've got to deduct two or three nights of hotel room fees from your profits, or they get a voucher for dinner at one of Opryland's nicer restaurants. The dealers get a bit competitive about the whole thing."

"The contest would be a neat introduction to my piece on this show." Molly shuffled forward along with the rest of the crowd hungrily waiting to serve themselves from the buffet. "I've got to come up with some real front-page material if I want to get that promotion to senior staff writer. I thought Matt Wilkinson would be there until he died, but he's decided to retire and hang out with his seventeen grandkids." Dreaming of her new byline, Molly indelicately stepped on her mother's heel. "Sorry, Ma! So . . . can you remember what some of the winning pumpkins from the past looked like?"

"Sure. Two years ago one of the Northeastern dealers won by carving the Boston Tea Party into an enormous pumpkin. The year before that was won by one of the textile dealers. Her jack-o'-lantern showed a woman in a rocking chair sewing a quilt. I remember she had somehow managed to carve a wedding ring pattern into the quilt. It was the most incredible carving job I'd ever seen—well, on a vegetable anyway."

All around them, those who had already gathered plates of food were convening near bar tables covered by papaya-colored linen cloth in order to hurriedly devour their dinner before perusing the contents of the show. Molly loved the feeling of anticipation that emanated around the enormous room. People were speaking with friendly animation as they bit into buttery corn bread or lifted heaping forkfuls of barbequed brisket into their mouths. Molly noticed that everyone appeared to be drinking the same orange liquid out of plastic margarita tumblers.

"Are those some kind of margaritas?" she asked Clara, wetting her lips at the thought.

"Mango Madness Margaritas." Clara nodded, smiling. "And boy, are they good. Even I like them, sweet as they are. Look! I can see a dish of enchiladas up ahead." She rubbed her hands together with glee. "No cheese cubes for us, my cupcake. Dig in!"

Molly piled her plate with two tostadas, a steaming corn-cob, a spoonful of refried beans, and a plump biscuit. She and her mother moved off to the side, shoveling the food into their mouths without speaking so that they could get a look at the show booths before the remainder of the swelling crowd finished their dinners. Before they could completely clear their plates, however, a tall, kind-faced man with a shock of white hair and a ruddy complexion appeared next to Clara and deposited a plate of pulled pork dappled with Tabasco and a puddle of watery slaw onto their table.

"Clara Appleby! Don't tell me you're back on the show circuit," the older man said, putting an arm around Clara's shoulders and squeezing with affection.

"No, Tom. I'm through with all that. I'm actually here on vacation, accompanying my daughter." Clara pointed at Molly. "She's a reporter for *Collector's Weekly*. Molly, this is Tom Barnett, one of the most honest dealers you'll ever meet.

He always has a spectacular inventory, and you don't have to be a professional athlete to be able to afford his prices."

"You're too kind," Tom said and shook hands with Molly.

"I've seen your ads in our paper," Molly said, wiping her mouth with an orange paper napkin. "You specialize in antique medical items, right?"

Tom smiled. "Yes. My shop's called the Country Doctor and I carry everything from apothecary chests to surgical cases." He took a swallow of mango margarita. "You'll see my pathetic attempt at representin' my shop when you see my pumpkin. I tried to carve a caduceus on it but it's no prizewinner, that's for sure." He issued a wry laugh.

Molly chuckled politely to humor the dealer. It was impossible not to like the pleasant man, but Clara's eyes narrowed as she quietly studied Tom. "I'm glad to see you here, Tom. Last time I saw you at this show you were in the middle of a divorce and your shop wasn't doing too well. Have things perked up?"

Tom shrugged and looked instantly weary. "I don't know about that. Ever since I started listin' on the Internet, sales have been real good, but my ex-wife is nothin' short of a holy terror. The U.S. Treasury doesn't print enough money to satisfy that woman. She'd sell my corpse for science without waitin' for me to die first." He took a deep swallow of margarita. "I guess it's the liquor makin' me feel so fine tonight. Makes me forget all my troubles and believe me, my dear, I've got a boatload." He hesitated, running a finger around the rim of his glass, "Along with these orange beauties, I also met a friend for drinks at the bar earlier so this isn't my first taste of hooch this evening." He smiled ruefully and then his smile instantly contorted into a grimace as he recognized someone behind Molly. "Gotta go! Here comes Charity, aka Demon-Woman. Stop by my booth later and we'll catch up," he said to Clara and hurried off, leaving most of his dinner untouched on the table.

"That was a quick exit," Molly commented and colleted their plates for the trash.

"That's because his ex-wife is heading over." Clara grabbed Molly's elbow and steered her in the opposite direction of the nearest trash bin. "I don't want to get in the middle of anything. She looks like a regular viper."

"Which one is she?" Molly tried to glance back over her shoulder. She was curious to see what a human viper looked like.

"The black-haired woman with the black dress. Looks like a witch. Uh-oh, she has her broomstick pointed this way. Let's go!"

Molly caught a quick glimpse of a woman in her mid-forties with shining black hair wearing an attractive calf-length cotton dress and a fierce scowl as she shouldered her way through the buffet line. A glimpse was all Molly got, however, as Clara dragged her away. As Molly passed by the dessert display, she saw an opening in the line and darted in, snatching a plate bearing a piece of yellow cake with chocolate icing like a moray eel striking out at its prey.

"Damn, I threw out my fork," she muttered to herself as they moved down the first aisle of dealer booths. Shifting the cake plate to one hand, she pushed her leather tote bag containing her camera and notepad higher onto her shoulder and then tried to tear off an end of the moist cake as her mother paused to examine a bucket bench in mustard paint.

"This would look nice on my front porch." Clara ran her hand over the surface of the pine bench. "Too bad we have no way to get furniture back home." She sighed theatrically. "Looks like we'll only be buying smalls on this trip."

As they progressed deeper into the booths away from the dining throng, Molly attempted to eat her cake without making too much of a mess, but just as she was admiring the Windsor chair carved into the jack-o'-lantern in a booth called Ye Olde Homestead, Clara nudged her in excitement and a chunk of frosting tumbled down Molly's chest.

"Ma! Look what you did!" She glared at her mother.

Clara tried to suppress a smile. "You could have waited until you had a fork. Never mind your sweater. We'll get it clean back in the room. Right now, I want you to see this game board. It would be perfect in your living room."

The board was a simple thing—a flat piece of wood bearing squares in cranberry and deep saffron paint. The squares were imperfect and the paint had flaked off in a few places, but even at its marked price of $595, Molly loved the piece. As she began to bargain with the dealer, who was hovering expectantly beneath a booth sign reading PAST TIMES, Clara examined a beautiful pie safe with incredible tins. Each of the six panels contained punched curlicues surrounding the profile of a proud rooster. Molly photographed the pie safe while dropping pointed hints to the dealer about her occupation and promising to add a line or two about the booth in her article on the show. As a result, she was able to walk away with the game board for the nicely reduced price of $475.

"You got a good deal on that." Clara tapped on the paper-wrapped board in approval. "One more row to go and I haven't fallen in love with anything."

"I'm sure something will catch your eye." Molly stopped to look at the price tag on a log cabin quilt hanging on the back wall of a textile booth named Geese in the Wind.

"Those are wonderful colors, aren't they?" the dealer asked. She had light brown hair that hung well past her shoulders in a cascade of soft waves, a friendly, heart-shaped face, and a full figure. She looked to be in her mid-thirties and was almost as tall as Clara. Molly returned her warm smile. "Gorgeous. I've never seen all of these hues of green, brown, and red put together. It would be a great display piece for Christmas."

Molly looked around at some of the other quilts. She recognized bear's paw, wedding ring, and the bow tie pattern, and marveled at how each quilt was fanned out across the three walls. Various quilts and coverlets were also spread over miniature beds, side chairs, and a group of table runners covered the top of an oak trestle table. Vibrant hooked rugs were scattered around the floor and rag doll animals such as black cats, dogs, and bears were propped around the booth in order to provide whimsical touches. Sprays of dried lavender hung from colorful threads high above their heads.

Between the scents and the soft lighting, Molly longed to curl up in one of the miniature beds and take a nap. In addition to the charming atmosphere within the booth, Molly was awed by the Baltimore Album quilt that had been carved into a gargantuan pumpkin. The intricate work must have taken hours to complete.

"Your jack-o'-lantern is amazing!" Molly complimented the dealer. "In fact, your whole booth is so artistically arranged that I'm forgetting that I'm in a hotel's convention center. Do you mind if I take some photos tonight and come back to interview you tomorrow about your booth design? I'm covering the show for *Collector's Weekly* and our readers would really enjoy seeing a creative display like this."

"I'd love you to. I could always use some free publicity and *everyone* reads your paper. My name's Becky Ross." She paused. "I know, I know. It's not Betsy, but close enough." Becky grinned, though she had probably repeated the corny phrase hundreds of times.

The booth neighboring Geese in the Wind couldn't have been more different. It had bright, halogen spotlights illuminating white walls covered with folk art paintings. Three tables with stark white cloths formed a U in the center of the booth. Folk art carvings and pieces of southern folk pottery were displayed in neat rows on each of the tables. The typed and laminated labels describing each piece revealed rather high price tags: Nothing was marked at less than $600.

The dealer was busy speaking with another customer, so Molly and Clara were able to examine each piece of folk art at their leisure. Clara was particularly fond of a primitively carved alligator, but she wasn't too crazy about the price marked on its label.

"It says here that this was carved in the mid-nineteenth century and was likely sold as a souvenir at one of Florida's gator farms," she said, reading the description typed on the label. "I guess people traveled down the East Coast to see the gators and in those days, that would have been a long and tough carriage ride. They wanted to return home with a unique souvenir of their travels. Sure beats a postcard." Clara picked up the gator and examined its painted smile.

"Here's a walking stick with a carved gator on the top, Ma." Molly pointed out another souvenir item held within a display case. "I like him, too."

Clara looked at the walking stick briefly, but she kept returning to the carved alligator, holding him in her hands as if he were a newborn infant. "No, if I buy anything at this show, it's going to be this wonderful piece. I know just the place for him at home. He can sit right on top of the blanket chest in green paint in the TV room." She smiled. "Can you even imagine what the cats will make of him?"

Molly shrugged. "If none of your *seven* cats have broken any of your pottery by now, then I think a wooden alligator should be perfectly safe." She finished her survey of the paintings and then took a quick glance around the circumference of the booth again.

"Hey, there's no pumpkin here," she whispered to her mother, who was taking in the vibrant colors of a painting done by Bernice Sims, the Alabama folk artist who began painting when she was in her fifties. This piece showed a group of African-American children hanging laundry on the line in front of a one-story house built in the traditional southern shotgun style. The figures of the children were replete with energy as they took to their chore. One of them, however, had strayed off to the left-hand side in order to play with a white-spotted dog. The piece was charming and whimsical.

"I love her work," Clara stated and then suggested that they move along. "I'll explain about the lack of pumpkin here later, but as we leave, take a good look at the dealer," Clara muttered, her voice barely audible as the booth began to fill with a fresh group of shoppers.

Just as they were leaving, the customer who had been busy scribbling out a check for a Jimmy Lee Sudduth painting of a red barn done in mud and house paints on a piece of rough wood board, ripped his check out of his checkbook and handed it to the dealer. The dealer, a slight man with salt-and-pepper hair, small silver spectacles, and a splint on his right hand, thanked his customer deferentially and slid the check into the front pocket of his brown corduroy pants. He then limped over to the other side of his booth, and using a soft and dignified voice, greeted the group of browsers. Molly noticed that he used an unadorned brown walking stick with an ivory or bone knob to help support the weight of his left leg. In the brief moments in which she studied the man, she felt that there was something pitiable about him, but she couldn't put her finger on what it was.

Safely inside the next booth, she plucked at her mother's sleeve. "That poor man! What happened to him?"

"What *didn't* happen to him is more like it." Clara lowered her voice as she pretended to be interested in an antique shooting target made out of cast iron featuring a pig with worn peach paint. "You can see, from his injured hand, that Dennis Frazier could never carve a pumpkin. And since he works alone, he just doesn't enter one in the contest."

"That name sounds familiar," Molly mused. "His sign says that he's from Chapel Hill, but I've never been to his store."

"His gallery is in his house, and only open by appointment. I think he has a small number of loyal and *very* rich clientele. His house is just darling. It's right off Franklin Street, within walking distance to the university campus.

He moved into it soon after his wife was murdered in their Raleigh home."

Molly's eyes widened in recognition. "Now I remember! I read about that in the paper, back when I was still teaching middle school. Wasn't he actually accused of the murder?"

Clara frowned. "He was a suspect. 'Course, the husband always is when the wife is murdered, though I can think of many more reasons for *wives* to be the ones committing violent crimes. . . ."

"Let's not get off the subject," Molly cautioned.

"No one who knew Dennis believed that he killed his wife. True, anyone could see that Dennis and Juliette didn't really get along, but he just didn't seem like the murdering type. The only passions stirring his blood were pieces of folk and outsider art. At auction, Dennis would have the same gleam in his eye as the rest of us, but otherwise, the guy was nice but pretty damned dull." Clara moved away from the shooting target in order to run her fingers along the surface of a wooden candle box. "Besides, he had been in a car accident a few weeks before her murder and sustained some horrible injury to his hand or forearm. I can't remember the specifics, but you can see for yourself that he's rather handicapped. Anyway, there wasn't enough evidence to bring him to trial. He spent a few unpleasant nights in jail before he was released."

"And the murder?" Molly asked, completely absorbed. "Was it ever solved?"

Clara stopped and furrowed her brows in thought. "No. I guess it wasn't."

Mother and daughter made their way to the end of the row. "Did you know his wife?" Molly inquired.

"Remotely. Juliette was a dealer, too, and a miserable woman. Haughty, spoiled, coiffed. She was the type with the perfect manicure, wardrobe, and shoes that cost more than your weekly grocery bill, and a waist that Vivian Leigh would have coveted, but Juliette repelled most of the people I know because she was always putting down American antiques." Clara sniffed, as if still offended by the very memory of the woman. "She was always going on about the superiority of French antiques. Called American things crude imitations and poor investments, if you can imagine such a travesty. And of course, primitives and folk art are Dennis's forte, so you can see why her criticisms might have grated on him as the years went by."

"How does a couple like that get together in the first place?" Molly turned toward an unattended tray fully stocked with mango margaritas. "They must have been aware of one another's likes and dislikes before they tied the knot."

Clara reached out for a glass. "Juliette had no money, but she was beautiful. Dennis was a plain-looking, successful man in his mid-thirties. She saw an advantage and so did he. They got married and then discovered that they couldn't stand one another." Clara took a swallow of margarita and shivered. "Ugh! These are too sweet for me after all. At least they had no children," she went on about the Fraziers. "I hate it when mismatched couples come to the brilliant conclusion that if they have a child, their marital problems will simply disappear, kind of like the margaritas sliding down Tom Barnett's throat."

Clara gestured toward a tray across the aisle. Tom Barnett drank down a margarita in three swallows and then quickly grabbed another. He seemed to be drinking more out of desperation than from a sense of enjoyment.

"Maybe we should see if he's okay," Molly suggested and Clara nodded in agreement.

As they approached Tom, they could easily see beads of perspiration dotting his forehead. Though the room was crowded, it was not unduly warm. No one else seemed uncomfortable or overheated. Tom's eyes darted wildly about, like a rabbit cornered by a hungry fox. They watched as he wiped his palms repeatedly onto his pants in a frantic, compulsive gesture.

"Tom!" Clara called out in what Molly recognized was her phony so-glad-to-see-you tone. "Shouldn't you be at your booth?"

"My assistant is there," Tom replied with agitation in his voice. "And she'd better sell a hell of a lot. Charity cornered me earlier today. Says she's takin' me to court for more child support." He took a deep gulp from a fresh margarita. "She's a human leech. She gets plenty from me already."

"Maybe you should concentrate on sales then," Clara said bluntly, pointing at Tom's drink, then softened her tone. "No one can sell your pieces like you, Tom." She clearly hoped the compliment would get Tom back on track, but he kept right on drinking. "You tell such marvelous stories about your items. I bought that jelly cupboard from you based on a story. Remember you said it had been used to hold bandages and other medical supplies during the last two years of the Civil War?"

Tom sighed, his forehead creasing with worry. "Thank you, Clara, but it's not just Charity. You see, I . . . I saw something today . . ." Tom looked about him as if he were being stalked. Molly was shocked at his fearful demeanor. "I shouldn't have seen, but I was in the wrong place at the wrong time and I *did* and now . . ." He quickly clamped his lips together.

"Tom?" Clara prompted, but the dealer merely drained his margarita and wiped at the sweat on his face with an orange napkin.

Before Clara could counsel Tom any further, a small man who looked exactly like the actor Nathan Lane but with a darker shade of brown hair and a neat goatee appeared beside their little group.

"Why, Clara Appleby. How divine!" He snatched Clara's hand and planted a kiss on the palm with a graceful flourish that only gay men and buccaneers can get away with. Noting the man's cantaloupe-colored silk shirt and creamy linen pants, Molly had to assume he was of the former category.

"Hello, Geordie." Clara hugged the Nathan Lane looka-like. "The show's wonderful! Molly, this is Geordie Alexis, the promoter."

"Charmed," Geordie said, blowing a quick kiss at Molly before turning his attention to Tom. The show promoter's flirtation immediately dissipated and in a tone that belied disapproval he pointed toward the hallway and said, "A word, Tom?"

Molly saw Tom tense and then nod his head in resignation. It appeared as though he was in Geordie's doghouse for some reason. As the two men stepped out into the hall through a set of closed fire doors, Clara dumped her unfinished cocktail into a nearby bin.

"Let's finish this last row. Tom's booth is here; you can see for yourself what wonderful items he has." She looked in the direction of the hall solemnly. "Or at least I hope he has. I think I'll ask Tom's assistant what's troubling him. I've never seen him like this before. It's unsettling."

Molly nodded mutely. As they approached the booth bearing the sign THE COUNTRY DOCTOR she said, "Tom really didn't look well physically. He was too sweaty and his hands were shaking. Do you think he's sick?"

"He will be if he doesn't sell some stuff tonight. All of these preview party people have their wallets stuffed full, just ready to buy," Clara stated as they entered Tom's booth. "Either way, that poor man is going to feel awful in the morning. I hope he's got an antique hangover cure somewhere in his inventory!"

Chapter 3

"Doctors carried vials of medicine and surgical instruments hidden in their system sticks . . . and when the doctor failed, the mortician carried a measuring stick in his to determine the length of his newest customer."

JEFFREY B. SNYDER, CANES AND WALKING STICKS:
A STROLL THROUGH TIME AND PLACE

The next morning, Molly woke to the sound of muttering coming from the hotel room's bathroom. Closing her eyes, she tried to ignore the throbbing around her temples, no doubt caused by too many mango margaritas the night before. If she had been by herself in the room, she could have slipped back into sleep. But she was not alone; Clara was awake and from the sounds she was making, attempting to work the room's four-cup coffeemaker.

"Oh good, you're up." Molly heard her mother's voice from across the room. She kept her eyes closed and her breathing regular, in the vain hope that Clara might leave her be to sleep a little longer. "Come on, I know you're awake." Her mother took a few steps closer to Molly's bed, not even bothering to whisper. "I can't get this stupid coffeemaker to work and it's almost seven. I've got to have some coffee while I watch the Weather Channel."

Molly groaned and opened one eye. Keeping half of her face buried in the pillow, she cast a scornful glare in her mother's direction and asked, "What do you care what the weather's going to be? We'll be inside all day at the show."

"Ha!" Clara pronounced triumphantly while settling herself at the foot of Molly's bed. "I *knew* you were up. And we're *not* going to be inside all day because this is a show on top of a show." Clara's dark gray eyes twinkled with excitement. "You see, there's a *huge* tailgate show attached to Heart of Dixie."

"You make it sound like a party," Molly said from beneath the covers.

"It is!" Clara swatted the mattress next to Molly's leg. "Every hotel room in the group of hotels across the street is full of dealers who didn't want to pay the booth rent for Heart of Dixie. So, those dealers sell out of the hotel lobbies and conference rooms. Unlike most other tailgate shows, they even sell right out of their private hotel rooms and from open cargo vans or card tables set up in the parking lot. And they put their wares out early, so get out of bed and fix that coffee machine, would you?" Clara put a hand on Molly's foot, which was covered by a layer of sheets and blankets. "Please, my dumpling. You know your old mama can't work complicated machinery."

Molly lifted her aching head and glanced at the clock. She had to pull it across the nightstand right up to her nose in order to read the blurred red digits. "Can't you wait ten more minutes? It's still six something."

Clara frowned. "Only for two more minutes. Up, up! I'm sure senior staff writers don't sleep late while on assignment, and it's a buyer's market out there. Do you want to miss the chance to discover some *rare* American treasure?"

"Of *course* not." Molly sighed, put on her glasses as her eyes weren't yet prepared to be invaded by contact lenses, and shuffled to the alcove outside the bathroom in order to examine the coffeepot. Her mother had correctly followed the directions, but the On/Off button seemed to be permanently stuck in the Off position. Molly checked to make sure that the pot was plugged in and then proceeded to reset the outlet. She tried switching outlet receptacles with the hair dryer, but nothing would coax the coffeemaker to life.

"The good news is that you're not mechanically challenged," she smugly informed Clara. "The bad news is that you're not getting any coffee from this machine . . . ever."

Clara handed the TV remote to her daughter. "That's unacceptable. You'll just have to go down to one of the lobby areas where free coffee is served and get us some. But first, be an apricot square and find the weather for your tired mother."

"Enough of that I'm-so-old-and-tired song and dance, okay? I'm already up, so you don't need to put on that act." Molly was exasperated as she surfed for the Weather Channel. Once Nashville's local forecast appeared on the screen, she went into the bathroom, wiped her face with a warm washcloth, and took three ibuprofen tablets. "Quick-release, huh," Molly muttered said as she examined the box. "They'd better be."

Pulling on a pair of jeans and her sweater set from last night, Molly finished off her outfit with a pair of flip-flops, which served as her slippers whenever she stayed at a hotel. "Just a drop of milk, right?" she asked Clara, seeking confirmation.

"Yes, thank you, pancake. And try to get the biggest cups you can find for both of us. You're not exactly a morning person, you know."

Molly had just opened the door when her mother added, "And stop by the front desk to complain about our coffeepot, too! Maybe we'll get a few more drink tickets," she called out hopefully.

Exhaling loudly in annoyance, Molly would love to have slammed the door, but it eased gracefully closed on silent hinges and she had to settle for repeatedly poking the elevator's down button in order to release some of her irritation at being sent for coffee when she should still be happily dreaming. When the elevator car arrived, it was empty. Molly descended to the lobby floor and was surprised at how quiet the enormous hotel seemed to be this morning. There were several groups of people already breakfasting at the Cascades, the restaurant overlooking the garden area not to be confused with the rotating lounge, and dozens of other guests bearing paper coffee cups were headed toward the lobby and afterward, the exit. Still, the majority of the Opryland's guests seemed to be asleep or relaxing comfortably in their rooms.

As Molly wandered over stucco bridges and followed a curving path adjacent to one of the gurgling streams, she completely forgot which direction would lead her to the Magnolia Lobby and the urns of free, fresh coffee. She noticed signs for the riverboat rides and realized that she had strayed out of the garden area and into the setting called the Delta. She was certain that she could find coffee for sale within the rows of shops but she hadn't brought cash or her room's key card with her, so she turned around and headed in a different direction, hoping to spy a sign that would direct her to either lobby. With almost 2,900 guest rooms, Opryland boasted two full-service lobbies, and Molly wished she could instantly materialize at the heart of one of them.

Crossing from the Delta into the space known as the Garden Conservatory, Molly paused in wonder. Lush tropical plants covered every square inch of ground while giant palm trees grew toward the glass ceiling. Stooping to admire a cluster of birds-of-paradise, Molly walked toward the atrium, where she had a clear view of a half a dozen footpaths and the miniature waterfalls flowing over stepped rock faces. As she headed north, a large party including several members traveling via wheelchair blocked her forward progress, so she veered off to the left, believing herself to still be headed toward the Magnolia Lobby. Unbeknownst to her, the path she was on turned gently west and then plunged downward to where the narrow stream was almost completely obscured by vegetation. Coming to a halt before a single garden bench, Molly sat down heavily and groaned. She was lost.

"I should have brought the map," she chastised herself. "Ma is going to kill me when I finally *do* show up with her coffee."

Even though she should be feeling frantic over being lost when she needed to get a jump on the day, it was just too early in the morning to become seriously agitated. The quiet garden setting was so calming that Molly longed to linger, so she sat down on a wrought iron garden bench. She listened to the sounds of water splashing as it echoed softly around the rafters and watched in amazement as two birds darted above her head, pieces of dried grass held captive in their beaks. She wondered what the plant growing alongside a grouping of Christmas cacti was called. It had wide green leaves covered by brown patches resembling a tortoise's shell and bore small white flowers on narrow stems.

Molly got up from her seat and crossed to the far side of the path. She squatted in order to read the small plaque positioned at the base of the unique plant. The sign informed her that she was gazing at a *Maranta (Leuconeura)*, whose common names were prayer plant and rabbit's tracks. As Molly stood erect, she noticed sunlight winking off a piece of glass nestled in an empty space between two oversized ferns growing behind the Maranta.

"That looks like a margarita glass," Molly said aloud in disgust. "Who would litter in such a beautiful setting?"

Stepping gingerly over the Christmas cactus with its crimson blooms, she moved several feet forward into the garden bed. Carefully, she picked her way among the ferns until she was within reach of the glass. Several yards beyond the ferns, the stream was mostly hidden by dwarf palms and a tall gathering of elephant's ear, which was a unique shade of purplish black. Molly retrieved the glass and then looked about her with amazement. Standing in the small oasis, she felt transported to a miniature rainforest. As she slowly pivoted her body and took a few more careful strides deeper into the bed, she noticed that the streambed was wider in this part of the garden and that there were no paths between where she stood and the hotel's interior walls.

"What the . . . ?" Molly suddenly stared at a gap between the elephant's ear. Her eyes fixed upon what appeared to be a black shoe, but what her mind could not quite digest was the bit of leg covered by an argyle ankle sock peeking out from between the waxy leaves of a large tropic snow plant. She walked closer, peeling back the fans of palm fronds that partially blocked her view of the stream. Beyond the bristled surface of the palm's trunk and the smooth boulder resting in its shade, Molly stopped short.

There, on the ground, partially hidden by several other varieties of tropical plants, a man was spread eagle upon the ground. The right half of Tom Barnett's body was submerged in the stream and the water lapped lazily over the brown chinos and green crewneck sweater that he had been wearing the night before. Tom's face was turned away from Molly, and the gentle stream flowed like a caress over his motionless features.

"Oh my god," Molly breathed and rushed forward. Kneeling beside him, she knew that taking Tom's carotid pulse was a useless gesture, for it was clear that his chest was no longer rising and falling, and that fresh, oxygen-rich blood hadn't brought color to Tom's cheeks for hours. Molly felt his cold neck and then backed away, grateful that the kind eyes of her mother's friend were closed.

Retreating from Tom's splayed arms, his pallid skin, and his partially submerged face, Molly stumbled back toward the bench. A dark-haired woman wearing a Gaylord Opryland polo shirt was unreeling a thin hose in preparation for watering the bed from which Molly suddenly appeared. The woman exclaimed something in Spanish and then jabbed a finger at the ground where Molly was on the brink of trampling some blooming nettles.

"Please," Molly said, her voice barely audible. "There's a body . . ."

She brushed by the startled gardener, sank down onto the bench, and tried to control her breathing. *"Hombre muerto,"* Molly panted, utilizing two of the dozen Spanish words she knew. She pointed toward the stream as the gardener stared at her suspiciously. Molly realized that she was still clutching the margarita glass.

"I'm not drunk!" she shouted breathlessly. "Dead man! *¡Hombre muerto!"* she repeated desperately, for the air around her had begun to feel stuffy and overheated and she could not seem to get enough of it into her lungs. The last thing she noticed was that the dark-haired woman removed the walkie-talkie from her belt and began speaking into it in rapid Spanish. Molly thought she recognized an accented version of the word *cadaver* before the green leaves around her knit together and began to spin faster and faster until they faded completely into black.

Chapter 4

When Molly came to she felt parched and more than a little embarrassed. She had only fainted twice in her life. The first time occurred during her freshman year in college when one of the nurses working in the visiting blood mobile had found it necessary to stick Molly's arm a dozen times in order to find a vein. Just as she was about to give up and walk out, the nurse struck a good vein but failed to hold the needle properly. It slipped from beneath Molly's skin and for a few seconds, blood squirted freely out of her left arm. It only took a quick glance for Molly to promptly pass out, but it took thirty minutes, six Oreos, and a cup of cherry Kool-Aid before she felt normal again.

The second time she fainted was during a recent assignment in Richmond, in which Molly had discovered the body of a murdered appraiser seated behind the wheel of his rental car. She had blamed that bout of swooning on the blazing summer sun, but this time she had to admit that it was more than humidity that had caused her to blackout.

Molly sat up slowly, keeping her eyes lowered, and accepted a damp towel from the female gardener. She pressed the cloth against her clammy forehead and instantly felt better. Still partially hunched over, she noticed that there was a man in an impeccable blue suit with shiny black loafers sitting beside her. He leaned forward so that he could peer into her face with a look of utmost concern. She caught a pleasant hint of aftershave, which seemed to aid in clearing her muddled brain.

"Are you all right, miss?" he asked, brushing a tiny white flower petal from the tip of his shoe.

Molly nodded. "I will be. I just need a second," she answered slowly, as if testing her ability to speak.

"Can I get you anything? Perhaps some orange juice? I think it's best if you remain still for the moment." He cleared his throat as if what he was about to say was difficult for him. "I've notified the authorities and I'm certain they'll want to speak to you. I am *terribly* sorry that you had to be the one to discover the . . . ah . . ." He trailed off, clearly at a loss for words.

Molly examined the man's brass pin listing his name and title in black script. "Thank you, Mr. Fallon. I think some juice would be great, and if you would, could you call my mother? She's waiting for me in our room."

The manager hesitated, undoubtedly wanting the shocking presence in the stream to become known to as few of his guests as possible. As Molly carefully sat upright, she noticed that both ends of the path had been roped off with maintenance tape backed by a row of yellow signs on stands reading CAUTION. WET FLOOR.

Sensing his reluctance to involve her mother, Molly added, "I think the police will want to see her, too. She knew the man in there." She pointed toward the stream and gave the manager their room number, leaving him no opportunity to argue. He got up and hurried away and Molly settled herself back on the garden bench.

Within five minutes, Fallon returned bearing a small tray with a glass of fresh orange juice and a buttered biscuit. He set the tray down beside Molly and then began to pace back and forth as he talked with quiet urgency into his cell phone. Molly had polished off both the juice and the delicious biscuit by the time her mother appeared, led by the same dark-haired gardener who had revived Molly after her faint.

Clara turned a pair of stormy eyes to her daughter. "What on earth is going on?" she demanded and then swung around to face Fallon. Assuming that he was a maitre d' or something of the sort, she said, "I sent my only child out for coffee forty minutes ago as the coffee machine in our room is *broken*. And she never came back! Do you think we could get a *whole pot* with some milk on the side?" She looked around in confusion until her gaze fell on Molly's crumb-laden tray. Clara beamed at the befuddled manager. "Oh! Can we order breakfast, too? My, this is *some* service you've got here."

"Umm . . ." the manager squirmed beneath Clara's penetrating stare.

"It would be *so* nice of you to arrange for coffee." Molly smiled sweetly at the agitated manager. "And then I can *quietly* explain to my mother what's happened." She lowered her voice to a whisper and leaned toward him. "The police will no doubt appreciate coffee as well." She added conspiratorially, "It doesn't hurt to start off on the right foot with them."

Fallon gave a dull nod and hustled off, issuing a few directives in Spanish to the gardener, who had remained amazingly nonplussed since Molly's discovery of the body.

"Did you say something about police?" Clara frowned, still looking around their setting in bewilderment.

Molly removed the empty tray from beside her and placed it on the ground. Patting the empty seat she said, "You'd better sit down, Ma."

Clara obeyed, examining her daughter's face carefully. "You look rather puny, as your grandmother used to say when I was coming down with something. What's going on?"

"Well, for starters, I got lost trying to find the lobby and I ended up here." Molly gestured toward the margarita glass sitting on the ground by the foot of the bench. "Then I saw that glass in the bushes and I went to pick it up—"

"What does that glass have to do with getting me my coffee?" Clara cut in before Molly could continue.

"There's a *man* back in those bushes, Ma," Molly plunged on, irritated with her mother's fixation on being denied her coffee. "He's dead. I saw his body when I went to get the margarita glass."

Clara took her daughter's hand in her own. "Oh, honey. How awful! No wonder you look so pale." She paused. "Was he old? Do you think he had a heart attack or something?" Without waiting for an answer, she continued. "Poor thing. Still," she looked around and smiled, "it's quite a tranquil place to die. Not a bad view if it's the last one you're going to see. Just look at those orchids over there. Gorgeous little things, aren't they? And do you smell that mint? It's so—"

"Ma!" Molly was exasperated. Shaking Clara's hand away, she pointed in the direction of the body. "You *knew* the dead man!"

Clara's gaze slid away from the orchids and fixed upon the verdant area Molly indicated with a shaky finger. "Oh," she said softly and then, "Who is it?"

"You can't see him from here," Molly assured her gently. "But it's Tom Barnett."

The medical examiner was first to arrive on the scene. He was a stocky man with a square jaw and unruly ash blond hair. He introduced himself to the manager as Berkley Butler, politely declined Mr. Fallon's offer of coffee, and asked to be shown the body. The gardener mutely beckoned for him to follow her but Berkley began to speak in Spanish and the two exchanged words until they passed out of sight to the place where Tom lay.

Ten minutes later, a carbon copy of Berkley arrived and introduced himself to the slack-jawed Mr. Fallon as Detective Reginald Butler. The only dissimilarity between the twin brothers was the detective's military-style buzz and the intensity of his gaze. After disappearing in the direction Berkley had taken, Detective Butler reemerged moments later and headed directly toward Molly.

"Good morning, ma'am." He shook hands with surprising gentleness. After waiting for Clara to introduce herself he handed Molly a business card. "I'm Detective Butler of Nashville P.D. I understand you were the one to find the deceased. Is that correct?"

"Yes," Molly answered. "At about twenty after seven."

The detective stared at her unblinkingly. "And how did you come to be so far off the beaten path at such an early time in the morning, if I may use a cliché?"

After offering the details of their broken coffeemaker and her sojourn for free coffee, Molly gestured at the margarita glass and explained how she had sought to retrieve it.

"Has anyone else handled the glass?" the detective asked. "After you picked it up?"

"No."

Butler drew a small notebook out of his jacket pocket. "And I understand you were able to identify the deceased. Could you tell me the nature of your relationship?"

Molly paused, trying to figure out how to verbalize her recent acquaintance with Tom Barnett. Clara filled the momentary silence by explaining how *she* had known Tom.

"So he's an antique dealer." Butler scribbled in his pad. "Here for the Heart of Dixie Show?"

"That's right," Clara replied.

Butler sighed. "This is my uncle Geordie's biggest event. He's not going to be pleased with any hitches this weekend." He rubbed the stubble on his chin thoughtfully. "What else can you two tell me about Tom's behavior last night? Did anything strike you as unusual?"

Clara and Molly exchanged quick glances.

"Lots!" Clara said dramatically. "But why are you asking about his behavior? Doesn't the man in the bushes—the one who looks just like you—know how Tom died?"

Detective Butler scowled. "It's for *me* to ask *you* the questions, ma'am, and these questions are strictly routine." He gesticulated with impatience toward the garden bed, where his twin worked. "Don't be concerned about my brother, Berkley. He's the finest medical examiner in all of Tennessee. He'll find out exactly how your friend died in a compassionate and expedient manner, but sometimes he can't tell simply by looking at a person. This is one of those times." His tone invited no argument or additional questions.

"*I'll* go over last night's events, Ma," Molly jumped in quickly before her mother could ruffle the detective's feathers any further. "You just chime in if I miss anything important."

"Hrrmph." Clara began to sulk and then immediately perked up at the sight of Fallon collecting a tray from a waiter who stood like an obedient dog on the far side of the maintenance tape. The tray bore a pot of coffee, three mugs, cream, and a plate of assorted rolls and Danishes along with butter and a jar of blackberry jam.

Clara poured coffee for all three of them and then buttered a croissant baked to a golden brown. Molly began her narrative of the previous night's events while eating small bites of an apple turnover. Detective Butler sipped his coffee and took notes in his pad. Two cups of coffee later, Molly had reached the part in the account when she and

Clara had visited Tom Barnett's booth toward the end of the evening.

When the Appleby women first stepped into the large booth space crowned by a wooden sign entitled THE COUNTRY DOCTOR, Molly had trouble absorbing Tom's disorganized displays. Antique surgery cases were scattered about on every available table surface among apothecary bottles and cases, leather-bound anatomy books, several yellowed casts of human skulls, and a full-sized skeleton wearing a Confederate officer's uniform. Dozens of canes were gathered haphazardly and stuffed into three umbrella stands.

A cane with a carved skull handle and a carved snake winding its way up the shaft intrigued Molly. She read the attached label with interest:

> Unusual Physician's System Stick. Late nineteenth century. Malacca shaft with carved snake. Skull handle made of bone, which unscrews to reveal hidden pomander jar so that the doctor could inhale a pleasant odor when faced with a noxious-smelling patient. Pomander jar lifts up to reveal two vials (both original with stoppers intact). The first contains laudanum (label missing) and the second, morphine pills. Beneath vials is glass flask that once contained whiskey. Missing stopper. Slight crack to the base of the skull. Ferrule is missing. **$750**

Molly examined the cane with great interest. She twisted off the skull and carefully removed the pomander jar. It was empty and held no trace of scent. One of the vials beneath it still read *Morphine Pills* in neat black script. The unlabeled whiskey flask looked like a modern test tube. She examined the damage to the skull and admired the carving of the snake. She made a mental note to talk to Tom further about the cane. It would make a perfect Christmas gift for Mark. Picking up several of the other physician's canes and walking sticks, Molly noticed that many of them had yet to be priced. As she made her way around the booth, it was clear that many of the smalls and several pieces of furniture had never been labeled or priced.

Molly paused to ogle a jar filled with glass prosthetic eyeballs marked at thirty dollars apiece, when a frumpy-looking woman with a round face and rosacea-reddened skin approached Clara and asked, "Can I help you?"

"We're just browsing," Clara replied, as her sharp gaze soaked in the scene of disarray. "It looks like Tom didn't even finish setting up," she stated bluntly. "And his booth has *always* been so well organized and easy to shop. What is going on with him these days?" She directed her question at the flustered woman, who must have been Tom's assistant.

"Um . . ." The woman groped for a suitable answer. She placed a nervous hand to the messy knot of graying brown hair gathered loosely at the nape of her plump neck and readjusted several bobby pins. This gesture added to the strain already being placed upon the buttons of her plaid blazer, which looked at least two sizes too small. Noiselessly, one of the jacket's brass buttons burst free of its tenuous thread, rolled the length of the booth, and settled beneath a blanket box nestled in the far corner.

Clara watched the trail of the wayward button with amused interest and then her eyes rounded as they met with the beautifully painted surface of the blanket chest. The front and side panels of the piece were a deep blue-green that had been decorated with soaring birds and bouquets of flowers in rich pigments of brick red, dark gold, and black. The colors had faded some with time, but the delicate brushwork on the primitive piece would speak volumes to any collector of Americana, of which Clara was one.

Stepping alongside Tom's assistant, who was headed in the same direction in order to retrieve her button, Clara tried to soothe the agitated woman. "I hate it when that happens. I don't think manufacturers use enough thread these days. I think it rolled under the right foot there." Clara pointed at the bottom of the chest helpfully.

"Thanks." The woman smiled. "I'm Darlene. I've been working with Tom for about six months." She examined Clara carefully. "It sounds like *you* know him well."

"Oh, I've been seeing Tom at shows for years. He also buys from Lex Lewis's Auction Gallery and I work there. I always call Tom when medical antiques are coming up for sale."

"So you knew him when he was still doing shows with his wife?" Darlene's face filled with curiosity as she got down on her hands and knees, displaying a pair of nude knee-highs with matching runs and an unattractive pair of brown orthopedic shoes. "He is *such* a sweet man. I don't see how he stayed married to *her* for so long," she practically hissed.

Clara was taken aback by Darlene's lack of discretion. Instead of commenting, she lifted the poplar lid of the chest and peered at the wood inside. "Pine," she said to herself.

Darlene finally closed her fingers around the button, sat back on her heels, and sighed. "Poor Tom. First his wife was harassing him and now that Geordie Alexis person is upset by how the booth looks. I'm worried about Tom's stress levels. He's had some heart trouble and is taking medication."

"Can't say that I blame Geordie for giving him a scolding," Clara mumbled under her breath, giving Molly a look. She then eased the small chest away from the wall in order to scrutinize the rough, unpainted back. Satisfied, she replaced it and squatted down in order to run her long and nimble fingers over the bracket feet.

"Late nineteenth century?" Molly asked her mother.

Clara nodded, her eyes riveted on the chest. "Yes. I'd say around 1880. It's Pennsylvania—definitely got a German influence. Most people would refer to it as a dower chest." She turned to Darlene. "I don't see a price tag. Can you look this piece up in Tom's inventory book? I'm quite interested in it, and he always keeps such detailed records."

Darlene stroked the sides of her hair and once again replaced several bobby pins as she cast a wild look toward the aisle, "Ah . . . Tom tucked the book somewhere earlier. He had some words with a man named Rose over that very piece of furniture and I haven't seen the book *or* Tom since." She sucked in a deep breath and plowed on. "But I'm *sure* he'll be back any moment now. He *knows* that I'm still pretty new at this and he's *very* kind to me."

Clara's look of annoyance was quickly replaced by one of curiosity. "Was the man *Howard* Rose? Of Rose Antiques and Auctions in New York?"

Darlene shrugged. "I don't know. He sounded like he had a New York accent, but to tell you the truth, he was so rude I could barely stand to listen to him. Poor sweet Tom. What a night he's had so far!"

Molly and Clara exchanged bewildered glances. Darlene seemed quite distraught over her boss's difficulties. "We'll check back in the morning," Clara promised. "In the meantime, you could probably help Tom out by arranging things a little around here."

"Do you think so?" Darlene's face lit with hope. "I'd do *anything* for him. He is just *such* a gentleman."

"She gushes more syrup than a Sno-Cone machine," Molly commented as they headed out of the show.

"Yes, she's clearly smitten with old Tom," Clara agreed. "Look! There he is now, and that *is* Howard Rose he's talking to."

Molly recognized Tom's profile as well as the prominent nose and dark, wavy hair belonging to one of the northeast's most successful antiques dealers. Rose's company was frequently highlighted in *Collector's Weekly* as it was consistently breaking records for achieving million-dollar sales during its quarterly auctions. Rose sold only high-end items and staked his reputation on the quality of the pieces to be found within his stores and on the auction block. Molly had never seen Rose in person however, and the powerful build of his body surprised her. Though neither tall nor broad, Howard Rose seemed to possess a compact strength beneath his custom Armani suit.

Clara marched straight toward the two men just as Howard was turning away. "This isn't over, Barnett," Howard said forcefully, his face dark with anger. "I'm taking that chest back to New York!"

"Over my dead body," Tom retorted and then walked off, looking rather unsteady on his feet as he disappeared around the corner of a booth.

A wicked grin sprouted on Howard's face. "Fine by me, country boy!"

Then, like some kind of magician, Howard vanished into the crowd.

Clara said, "My, my. I wonder what *that* was all about. It sounds like Tom is refusing to sell Howard that blanket chest."

Molly shrugged in bewilderment. "We can ask him later. Do you want to stop by Grayson Montgomery's booth on our way out, or do you want to check your hair and makeup first?"

"Not tonight, I'm beat." Clara sighed, ignoring her daughter's teasing. "Let's go upstairs and get into our pajamas. Maybe there's some wonderful old mystery on TV."

"That's the whole story," Molly concluded as she watched the detective's face for any reaction. Receiving none, she turned to her mother. "Did I forget anything?"

Clara shook her head and also fastened her eyes on Detective Butler as he compulsively rubbed his chin and stared down at his notes. Just as he was opening his mouth to speak, Berkley appeared from within the garden bed, zipped up what looked like a camera bag, and waved his brother over. The twins held a conference in hushed tones and then Berkley flipped a coin. He smiled smugly as he showed the result on his open palm; Detective Butler grimaced. Passing a meaty hand over the top of his spiky hair, he tapped his watch face and sighed. His brother issued an amused shrug and after offering a sympathetic glance, headed up the path.

"I'll be back with the gurney," he called over his shoulder as he marched off, Mr. Fallon dogging his heels.

"What do you think those two were trying to decide?" Clara whispered.

"I'd guess that the detective will have to tell Uncle Geordie that one of his dealers isn't coming back to the show," Molly replied somberly. "Ever."

PARIS, 1853

Pierre Avide slammed his fists upon the gleaming ivory keys of his piano and let loose a string of expletives.

"I specifically instructed that no one was to disturb me!" he yelled, hoping that the butler and footmen were cowering in fear.

The gilt-covered double doors leading to his music room opened and the powdered face of Pierre's paramour appeared, smiling devilishly at her lover's show of temper.

"Darling," she purred, crossing the room in a swish of silk skirts. Her heady perfume reached Pierre before she stretched out a long and elegant arm with which to caress his wavy brown locks.

"Claudine. I am preoccupied." Pierre said while rudely remaining at his seat before the piano. He turned away from her in vexation. "Both Liszt and Chopin will be coming to dine tonight and they have insisted that I perform for them. Master Liszt has finally conceded that he has never seen more gifted hands than these." Pierre held out his beautiful white hands and fluttered his long, white fingers as if they were the feathers on a dove's wing and not the mere flesh belonging to a bastard son of a nobleman.

"Yes, my sweet." Claudine settled herself on a chair in front of the fire and daintily arranged her voluminous skirts. "You have told me of your ambitions more than once: that you shall be the only man of your tender years to perform solely for members of royalty."

Swiftly, Pierre took to his feet and strode across the room. Tight-lipped, he grabbed Claudine's elbow and glared at her. "I have sixteen years and there is nothing tender about me. I was meant for greatness and I will not waste my talent on even the richest members of the nobility."

Claudine grinned and shook her elbow free. "You are surely destined for fame and glory and that is why I chose you for my lover, you silly boy." She snapped her fingers in command and a maid carrying a paper-wrapped parcel rushed into the room, laid the package at the slippered feet of her mistress, bowed, and then scampered off again. "I have brought you a gift."

Pierre sank into the chair opposite Claudine and began to sulk. "I have all the gifts I need," he asserted flatly.

"Do you not wish to be known as the Musician to Kings?" Claudine leaned forward, her ample bosom straining against the tight confines of her gown. Pierre could not help but focus on the translucent skin that covered the round swells of his lover's breasts. His lust rising, he turned to her. "And?" he asked, still petulant. "What of it?"

"Well, you already possess many symbols of kingship. You have jewels fashioned with the images of lions, furniture carved with splendid suns, a coach emblazoned with your family crest . . ." She waved her hand as if these meant nothing. "But I have brought you the King of Snakes and he possesses a powerful secret."

At last, Claudine had managed to capture Pierre's interest. He grabbed the wrapped parcel from where it lay on the *woven rug and roughly tore off the paper. He stared at the wooden stick, his face reflecting his disappointment as he pivoted the carved cobra head to and fro before the firelight.*

" 'Tis simply a wooden stick. No jewels, no gold, not even ivory carvings. It's nothing but a hunk of wood!" He tossed the cane to the floor. "Some King of Snakes! This isn't even suitable for one of my servants to wear."

Claudine picked up the cane and began stroking the open-mouthed serpent on the handle. "Oh, it is more than a simple stick, my precious. It is a weapon as well. It has already caused the deaths of two people in Germany."

Pierre's eyebrows rose. "Truly? But how? It is not even useful as a bludgeoning instrument." Turning his back to her, he strode to the sideboard and poured himself a goblet of fine claret from a crystal decanter. Then, posing against the piano, he raised the glass to his lips without offering his guest a share of the refreshment. "I'm waiting to be enlightened."

"There is a blade hidden within the stick." Claudine spoke in an animated, husky whisper. "But the merchant I purchased the stick from was not wise enough to be able to discover its mysterious workings." Her face glowed. "That is also how the murderer escaped punishment for his crime. None could prove how this wood stick was able to slit the throats of his wife and her lover. Yet both were found with their own lifeblood pooling around their naked bodies, stab wounds visible upon their necks."

Pierre snatched the cane from her hands. "Surely a musical genius such as I can discern the primitive workings of a peasant's carving. The murderer was a peasant, was he not? No person of consequence would create such an atrocious stick."

"According to the merchant, he was a poor and uneducated smith. Still, he seems to have bested many men in terms of his little creation." Claudine moved closer to Pierre and pressed her body against his. "Why don't you put that stick aside for the time being?"

Pierre frowned. "Later, Claudine. I must . . . I would like to examine your gift, dear heart. Allow me to call upon you once I have solved its riddle." He deftly kissed her hand and then led her to the door. "Until tonight. And thank you for the present. You are a most remarkable woman."

Claudine smiled tenderly and allowed herself to be ungraciously dismissed. Once outside, a footman helped her into a black carriage pulled by a matching pair of gray mares. Within its plush interior awaited the famed composer, Franz Liszt. As soon as the carriage pulled away from the Avide estate, Liszt held out his arms to Claudine. She moved into his embrace.

"So all is well?" he murmured into her perfumed hair.

"That fool will be too preoccupied with the snake cane to properly prepare for his concert tonight. You have naught to fear, love. You will retain your absolute genius in the eyes of Chopin and the rest of Paris. When you return to Weimar, you can continue to compose without worry."

Liszt's handsome mouth curved into a smile. "And the tale behind the cane? Is it pure fallacy?"

Claudine shrugged indifferently. "Who knows? The merchant insisted upon the story of the murders as truth. Yet, my husband looked over the cobra's head inch by inch and saw nothing. Usually, he has a keen eye for such mechanical devices. No matter. Pierre's composure will be completely rattled when he fails to discover its secret. He does not play nearly as well when his attention is divided."

"That is good news indeed. And as for your husband, if he can not see what goes on right under his nose . . ." Franz teased as his deft fingers began to unlace Claudine's gown.

"I am pleased to see that you are suitably grateful, maestro, for I do not think I could stand another moment pretending to be that horrible, spoiled boy's mistress," Claudine complained.

"No, my love. You are meant to be the mistress of a

much more appreciative musician," Franz murmured and then fell to kissing his lover's neck and full mouth as the coach proceeded down the dirt track toward Claudine's chateau.

Pierre had completely set aside all thoughts of Claudine and of the importance of the evening's recital as he studied the snake-handled stick. Closing his eyes, he drummed his fingers lightly along the length of its shaft beginning with the top and moving carefully to its narrowed tip.

"There is a space within," he breathed in excitement after hearing the slightest reverberation inside the upper part of the shaft.

Hastily retrieving a silver-handled magnifying glass from his father's study, Pierre told his butler that he was not to be disturbed under any circumstances. "And if you disobey me in this order again, you will find yourself out in the streets!" he snapped as he slammed the doors to the music room closed.

Once he was comfortably reestablished in his chair before the fire, Pierre greedily gulped down the rest of his claret and poured himself another generous glass. Wiping his stained lips with his linen cuff, he began to examine the carved scales on the cobra's body one by one.

After almost an hour of intricate perusal, Pierre saw nothing out of the ordinary. Cursing, he drank down another glass of claret and began to press down on each scale with his index finger. Again, he closed his eyes and brought the stick next to his ear as his fingertips moved with agonizing slowness along each scale. Pierre paid little attention to the advancing minute hand of the brass carriage clock on the mantel as he probed the surface of the wood. Finally, his concentration was rewarded. One of the scales on the back of the cobra's neck gave way to the gentle pressure of Pierre's finger.

"Ah!" Pierre exclaimed exultantly, opening his eyes and peering at the scale. He pushed on it with more force. Nothing happened. "Damn you!" Pierre shouted at the stick, and flecks of spittle fell upon the cobra's white eyes. Pierre drank a fourth glass of wine and began to pace back and forth, all the while staring at the snake's frozen, open-mouthed hiss in defiance.

By now, Pierre should have completed practicing the concerto he was to perform within the next hour. He should have been upstairs, dressing in his finest attire in order to create a favorable impression not only upon the two composers Franz Liszt and Frederick Chopin, but upon his own father as well. Pierre's father saw him as a useless dandy who would never contribute anything positive to the family name. Duke Avide had proclaimed more than once that Pierre had only been recognized as the heir because the Duchess seemed to only be capable of producing "a litter of females." Luckily for Pierre, his late mother, his father's former mistress, had been able to give birth to a healthy male and Pierre was immediately taken into the Avide household and raised as a nobleman.

Despite all that was at stake, Pierre was so consumed in triumphing over the snake that he saw neither the death of the natural light beyond the windows nor heard the chimes of the mantel clock, warning him that his time to prepare grew dangerously short. Covering the snake's entire head with his right hand, Pierre depressed the scale on the back of its neck and recommenced poking at the scales on the underside of the stick using his left hand.

Pierre sank into the plump cushion of his chair and closed his eyes. He called up the memory of his favorite piano sonata and focused on the silent melody in his mind as his fingers searched the reptile's scales. He listened to the sound of his fingertip on each scale more intently than he had ever listened to a note of music. Just as he was about to concede defeat, his middle finger met with a slight give as he pressed upon a scale directly beneath the cobra's chin.

With his right hand still blanketing the back of the cobra's head, Pierre deliberately pushed upon the chin scale as forcefully as he could. A stiletto shot through the snake's head, piercing Pierre's hand and neatly severing the nerve between his thumb and index finger. For a moment, Pierre could only stare at the blade sticking out of his flesh. But as soon as he removed his left hand from the cobra's chin, the blade instantly retracted, leaving Pierre to watch in horror as blood bubbled out of the hole in his right hand. He began to scream for help, feverishly wrapping his bleeding hand with a lace handkerchief.

When no one came to his aid, he stumbled outside the music room and shouted hysterically, "HELP ME! HELP ME!"

A bevy of servants came running and Pierre was half-carried to his feather bed. He was given a measure of brandy and a footman dashed off to fetch the doctor. While all of this was occurring, the butler, who had a propensity for listening on the other side of closed doors, stealthily entered the music room and collected the cobra cane. He eyed the stick curiously, saw not a trace of blood upon it, then carried it to the front hall. He placed it carefully in the umbrella rack along with a half a dozen other walking sticks and returned to his duties.

The doctor arrived in due haste and despite his best efforts, mournfully proclaimed that Pierre would never play the piano again. His right hand would henceforth be crippled as a result of the severed nerve.

The concert for the evening was cancelled and many days later, as Pierre lay abed, Duke Avide asked the butler to fetch him the instrument of his son's musical demise. When the butler scurried off to retrieve the cane from the umbrella stand in the front hall, it was gone.

Chapter 5

Detective Butler requested that Molly and Clara meet him downtown at the police station so that they might provide formal statements. Molly explained that she was in Nashville on assignment and promised to be at the station once the antique shows had closed down for the day. After collecting their room number and cell phone numbers, the detective seemed satisfied with their arrangement and then shooed them off as his brother arrived, carefully wheeling a gurney down the curved pathway.

Molly had no desire to lay eyes upon Tom's lifeless face again, so she pulled a hesitant Clara away from the garden area and back to the elevator bays that would take them to their room. Once inside their spacious bathroom, Molly immediately took a long, hot, luxurious shower. She used greedy amounts of the free products provided by Gilchrest & Soames and tried to process the surprising events of that morning. Once she had finished drying her hair, she felt almost human again, as though she had been washed clean of the heavy weight that had accompanied her discovery of Tom's body.

As her mother claimed her turn in the bathroom, Molly dialed the cell phone number belonging to her boss, Carl Swanson. Even though she had experienced some level of shock, she was still a reporter and Swanson would want to be apprised of the sudden death of one of the Heart of Dixie dealers.

"I'm fishing!" her boss barked into the phone by way of greeting. "And you just scared away my bass, Appleby!"

"Sorry, Carl," Molly replied, trying to keep a smirk out of her voice. "But I wanted to let you know that Tom Barnett, the owner of the Country Doctor, passed away this morning."

"At the start of Heart of Dixie?" Swanson silently pondered the news; Molly could only hear him breathing on the other end of the phone. Finally, he coughed and said, "Poor sucker. It's always been one of the biggest shows of the year for him. Shoot, we wouldn't get half of his advertising dollars without the sales from that show. Guess that's the end of his ads altogether." He paused. "What'd he die of?"

"I don't know." Molly stalled, not wanting to tell Swanson any details about the undignified state of Tom's demise.

"Then who told you he was dead?" Swanson growled.

"Um, I kind of found his body this morning. It looks like he collapsed in one of the garden beds here in the hotel," Molly said and then winced. She knew her boss would pump her for information in search of a dramatic angle to lend to her piece on Heart of Dixie.

"In a flowerbed?" Molly heard the distinctive click of a cigarette lighter. Swanson inhaled deeply and then said, "We should get a full memorial piece on him in Monday's edition. Everyone on the East Coast knew Tom, and I want to beat that rat bastard at *Fine Antiques Journal* to *this* front-page story."

Molly sighed. Her boss and Prescott Perry, the editor-in-chief of the *other* major antiques and collectibles paper, had been rivals for years. Recently, one of Prescott's writers had scooped a major story about an art forgery ring operating out of Maryland right from under the nose of a *Collector's Weekly* staff writer. That writer had been demoted to auction reports until he came up with a story big enough to capture the front page *and* the envy of Prescott Perry. Molly sensed that her boss believed that *she* might be holding the key to such a story.

"Now, I like Tom just as well as other folks, but we might have to sling a little mud to boost our sales," Carl began as Molly groaned softly. "You'll have to get a hold of his ex-wife."

"She's actually here, working the show for a friend," she was forced to admit.

"Perfect! Make sure you get some juicy quotes from her. None of this 'I'm going to miss him,' or 'He was a good man' crap." Carl inhaled deeply. "We're going to get those cheesy lines from every dealer who knew Tom as is. I want to paint a *full* picture of what life is like for someone who was able to survive in this miserable, ungrateful business for almost thirty years. I'll do the man justice, but his piece can't all be sunshine and roses."

"From what I understand, he actually *was* a good man," Molly retorted. "Are you smoking? I thought you quit," she added, feeling combative.

"Only when I'm fishin' and my wife's not here to see me. Now, get off my phone line and write me a front-page piece. Your show coverage piece can wait until midweek, so make Tom Barnett your top priority," Swanson said and hung up.

Clara opened the door leading to the balcony and stepped outside, hairbrush in hand. As she began to brush her thick hair, she gestured at their breathtaking view with her free hand. "I think we should go ahead with our weekend. I feel terrible for poor Tom, but there's no sense mop-ing about this hotel room. It won't bring him back to life." She grew quiet, absorbing the comforting white noise cre-ated by the waterfall below them. The door to the balcony next to theirs opened and a young woman stepped out, speaking in hushed tones on her cell phone. As if a spell were broken, Clara beckoned Molly to follow her back in-side their room. "The way I see it is this. You've got an ar-ticle to write and I'd still like to see what gems the dealers across the street have brought . . . *if* there's anything good left. Do you feel up to proceeding with our day as planned?"

Molly watched her mother swish mouthwash around her cheeks. "I do, but we should stop by Tom's booth be-fore we go."

Clara spit into the sink. "What on earth for?" she asked with abruptness.

"I think we should tell Darlene what happened to Tom, if no one has already. She's going to take the news pretty hard."

"She'll have a complete meltdown no matter who tells her," Clara mumbled as she applied lipstick. "I don't see why it should be us."

Molly took hold of her mother's elbow and spoke to her reflection in the mirror. "Come on, Ma. It's the right thing to do. Besides I've decided to buy that physician's cane in Tom's booth for Mark. The one with the snake and the hid-den vials. Christmas is only two months away and I'll never find a gift like that at the mall."

Clara gave her daughter a reproving glance as she shouldered her purse and opened the door to their room. "That's a lot of money to spend on a boyfriend. Now, if he were your *fiancé,* then I could understand. Of course, a di-amond would be a fair trade for a walking stick." Walking briskly down the hall, she jabbed the elevator button. "When are you going to get that boy to propose?"

Molly rolled her eyes and pressed the elevator button herself. "It's only our second Christmas together. Sure, I'd love to find a little square box in my stocking, but I'm not going to press Mark by issuing an ultimatum. He . . . he does things in his own time and lately he's been really busy." She didn't tell her mother that Mark had been preoccupied to the point of being negligent because she didn't want Clara to think her relationship with Mark was in jeopardy. If she didn't voice her fears than it was easier to pretend that they didn't exist.

The elevator car finally arrived and the doors opened to reveal a young couple embracing. Clara seemed to forget all about the subject of marriage as she fished around in her purse for a stick of gum, her mouth set in a frown of disapproval. Relieved, Molly whispered, "Let's focus on how we're going to tell Darlene that her boss is dead."

Inside the show, most of the dealers were busy rearranging their booths or unpacking fresh inventory due to a high volume of sales during the preview party the evening before.

Molly couldn't believe the change that had occurred in the Country Doctor booth. It was as though a group of fairies had appeared during the night and magically cleared the cluttered surfaces and artfully arranged the items in eye-catching and orderly displays. Darlene was placing a planter filled with cheerful yellow mums on the rough-surface of a pine farm table as they approached. A grouping of surgical cases had been arrayed in a fan pattern and covered most of the tabletop. Molly stared at three framed antique medical prints portraying a human skeleton in a variety of limber poses propped up in a precise row behind the surgical cases. In each print, the skeleton seemed to be wearing a smug and toothy grin, which unnerved Molly. Transfixed, she stood motionless as her mother put a hand on Darlene's shoulder and whispered gently to her.

Molly expected Darlene to burst out into boisterous tears upon hearing that Tom was dead, but instead, she sank noiselessly into a nearby metal folding chair, heedless of the paperback or cellophane-wrapped muffin that were now squished beneath her bottom.

"I *knew* he was too stressed!" she declared as she accepted a tissue from Molly, who was holding a stack in her hand just in case. Darlene blew her nose with a gooselike honk and then fanned herself with her right hand. "Between his ex and that Rose man and that perfectionist Geordie person, it's no wonder Tom's poor heart quit on him!" Tears began to flow from her eyes and roll undeterred down her round cheeks. "What will *I* do now?" She looked at Clara beseechingly. "How am I going to handle *this*?" She waved her arm around the booth. "Should I close the booth? How could I get it all packed up?" She fanned herself with more vigor. "Should I stay open and sell what I can? I think Tom would want me to," she babbled on, becoming increasingly worked up. "But I don't even know what prices to put on the unmarked items! Tom's inventory book isn't here. Maybe it's in his room. Maybe he—"

"We'll help you price these things," Clara interrupted firmly. "The inventory book would have been helpful, but I am confident that I know the fair market value of most of these items. Geordie will insist on you staying open for appearance's sake, so we might as well get busy. Now, wipe your face, put on some lipstick, and hand me a pile of tags. Molly and I will have this booth ready for when the doors open at ten."

Darlene nodded mutely and handed Clara a box of white tags and a black ballpoint pen. She had ceased fanning, but remained in her chair, where she sniffled and dabbed repeatedly at her eyes with the mangled tissue.

"Tom would really appreciate you being so strong right now," Molly said, giving Darlene a fresh tissue. "With his reputation as an honest dealer and a fine gentleman, you'll probably sell everything in this booth. Just think what a tribute that would be to Tom."

Darlene sucked in a giant breath, nodded, and gave Molly a weak smile. "You're right. I owe it to that dear, *dear* man to do my best in *his* name. Thank you both for being so kind."

"And, it just so happens that I'm your first customer this morning." Molly returned the smile. "I'm going to buy this physician's cane for my boyfriend." Molly removed the stick from the umbrella stand and placed it gingerly on the table in front of Darlene. "Why don't you write me a receipt while I help Ma with the pricing?"

"I know that Tom would have given you a discount, being that he and your mama were friends." Darlene examined the $750 price on the cane's tag, her demeanor becoming more businesslike as she spoke. "How does $595 sound? Will you be paying by check?"

Molly scribbled out a check and then tied price tags onto pieces of furniture, several canes, a few leather-bound anatomy books, and a phrenology skull made of painted ceramic.

"All done." Clara looked around the booth. "Luckily, Lex had a huge medical antiques auction this summer so I knew what the current prices should be." She turned to Darlene. "Tom usually gave a 10 percent discount to most people who asked, but you should leave that to your own discretion. And don't worry, we'll be back to check on you this afternoon. From the way you've arranged this booth, I'd say you were a *natural* at this profession."

Darlene sat up straighter in her chair. "Truly? Maybe I *can* finish this show alone. Tom would have been *so* pleased." She hesitated. "You *will* come back to check on me though, won't you?"

"Absolutely." Molly gestured at the cane she had just purchased. "As a matter of fact, I'm going to leave that here with you and come back for it after lunch. We'll bring you a tasty snack and I'll cover for you if you need to take a break. Bye now!"

"Well, that's enough kindness for one day," Clara announced as she and Molly left the show room and headed toward the lobby. "It might be necessary to get downright nasty since we're not the early birds at the tailgate show. That means if there's anything left worth buying, we're going to have to fight over it."

Molly chucked her mother in the arm. "Settle down there, Sugar Ray."

Outside, a gray sky was reluctantly giving way to pale blue and the air felt crisp. Walking alongside the long driveway leading to the front entranceway, the Appleby women were passed by dozens of taxis, rental cars, and small tour buses crammed with groups on their way to visit the Hermitage or gawk at the homes belonging to local country music stars.

By the time the two women had risked their lives crossing McGavock Pike, they were overheated and thirsty. However, as soon as they made their way inside the hotel directly across from Opryland's entrance, they forgot all about their discomfort. Satisfied shoppers carrying every conceivable collectible from folded quilts to shaker boxes to framed samplers marched through the automatic doors wearing pleased smiles.

"Oh no!" Clara wailed, doubling her pace. "We're getting such a late start!"

Molly knew better than to respond. She followed her mother as Clara stuck her elbows out like a flustered hen and cut a swath through the departing customers. Card tables with multicolored tablecloths filled the lobby and every conference room within the hotel. Around the perimeter of the atrium, all of the hotel rooms stood with doors thrown wide open, inviting shoppers to enter and peruse the dealer's stock within.

At the first open hotel room, Molly and Clara separated. Molly wanted to see what kind of stock was displayed within the individual rooms while Clara sought a pewter seller who set up every year within the maze of dealers renting bona fide booths inside the atrium.

At first, Molly felt extremely self-conscious about entering the hotel rooms. In many cases, the dealers had shoved the beds against the walls and rearranged the furniture in order to display as much of their inventory as possible. Vintage textiles were spread out over the unattractive hotel bed coverlets and several pieces of old oak furniture were tagged for sale amid the nondescript nightstands, television cabinets, and polished bureaus that were in every one of the hotel's ninety rooms. Every inch of visible surface area in this particular room-turned-booth had been covered by pieces of cut glass, china plates, platters, teacups, and rows of porcelain figurines.

The dealer was a woman in her seventies who used a walker to eagerly shuffle across the burgundy carpet in order to answer a customer's question about a Royal Doulton mermaid figurine.

"She's got a little chip to her tail, but she's old," the dealer said, pointing a finger at the figurine. "Saw one sell on eBay for just over four hundred bucks."

"Any discount?" the customer inquired, turning the mermaid over in his hands.

"I'll knock off twenty-five, but that's it. I got to pay for this room for three nights and rates ain't as cheap as last year."

After receiving payment in cash, the dealer adeptly nestled the mermaid in a layer of bubble wrap followed by several sheets of newspaper. The customer left with his purchase and Molly spent a few moments interviewing the dealer about the ups and downs of setting up across the street from the main venue. She then wandered from hotel room to hotel room examining a range of goods so varied that she felt like she was at a yard sale in Room 212, her grandmother's cluttered attic in Room 301, and a high-end Charleston antique shop in Room 368.

After interviewing several dealers and a handful of buyers, Molly made her way to the atrium. She was greatly surprised to discover her mother, comfortably seated in a Windsor armchair located on the edge of a booth called the American Charger. Enormous stepback cupboards were stuffed with pieces of antique American pewter. Clara was cradling an antique inkwell in her hands as she listened to a woman seated in a Windsor rocker. Molly couldn't tell who the woman was as she could only see the back of her head of dark hair, but as she drew closer, the woman pivoted slightly and Molly thought she recognized the face of the former Mrs. Tom Barnett.

"There you are!" Clara called out to Molly as if scolding her. "I've been having a nice talk with Charity Barnett. Charity, this is my daughter."

Charity was wearing a very different expression than the scowl Molly had seen on her face the previous night. Her eyes were shot with red and her long fingers trembled as she raised a delicate lace handkerchief to her ruddy nose. "Excuse my appearance," the woman apologized. "I've been wandering around this hotel like a zombie. Luckily, your mother came along and got me to sit down and get a grip." She looked at Molly, her deep blue eyes filled with sadness. "I understand you were the one to discover Tom this morning. That must have been quite a shock, finding him in the garden like that. My Lord." She shook her head wearily and stared unseeing at the parade of shoppers moving by. "As annoyed as I was with him last night, as on so many other nights, it's not the kind of death he should have had." After a stretch of silence, she added, "It was, well, pretty undignified."

"When was the last time you had something to eat?" Clara gently asked.

Charity seemed startled by the question. "Last night, I guess. I was just having coffee in my room this morning when the police came to tell me about Tom." She kept her gaze locked on the passersby. "After they left, I drove over here and just starting meandering."

Clara nodded her understanding. "Let's all get something to eat. I'm sure you could use the company right now and I heard there's a terrific cheeseburger joint downtown." Clara stood, rolling the pewter inkwell in tissue paper and placing it inside a paper bag. Waving to the booth dealer, whose nose was deep in a book, she put a hand on Charity's arm. "Come on, I think you could use a break from this hustle and bustle."

Molly threw her mother a perplexed look. It was unlike Clara to display such concern for a stranger. Clara returned the look with a silent appeal and Molly began to wonder whether her mother's kindness had an entrepreneurial motive. She sensed that Clara was sizing up Charity with the hope of winning the contract to sell Tom's estate once the lawyers had finished up with its division. Molly knew that items belonging to well-known antique dealers or collectors tended to bring good prices at auction, so it was no wonder Clara wasted little time in sticking her long and narrow foot in the door.

"We don't have a car, Ma," Molly said, and then, in an attempt to dissuade her mother from circling the new widow like a turkey vulture that has spied fresh carrion, whispered, "Don't you think you should at least wait for the funeral before you pounce on the widow."

"Excuse me?" Charity said, turning around, blinking as if clearing cobwebs from her eyes. "Did you say something?"

"Oh," Molly stammered, "just that I'm on the verge of getting a blister on my left heel. I think we'd better head back to our hotel for lunch."

Clara glanced dismissively at her daughter's shoes. "That'll teach you to wear boots that haven't even been broken in. You should be wearing sneakers."

"I've got a car parked right outside," Charity offered before the Appleby women could get their argument further off the ground. "And I *could* use some real food right about now. There's only one place to go in Nashville for burgers and shakes, and that's Ellison's. There will probably be a line 'cause it's Saturday, but the food is worth the wait. Shall we give it a shot?"

The appeal in Charity's voice was unmistakable. Molly nodded in acquiescence and Clara harrumphed triumphantly in her daughter's ear.

Ten minutes later, Charity skillfully parallel parked her rental Lincoln across the street from the restaurant. There was a simple glass storefront covered by a red-and-white-striped awning and black-and-white signs denoting the soda shop's daily specials. Nothing about the exterior was an indication of the small establishment's fame. However, at least a dozen people were lined up outside the front door, chatting in a relaxed fashion as if they were more than happy to wait twenty minutes in order to be seated. Molly and Charity joined the end of the line while Clara claimed she needed to use the rest room. Within moments, she reappeared outside the door and waved.

"Come on!" she beckoned. "They've got a table for us!"

Trying to ignore the surprised and irritated looks cast by those still waiting in line, Molly lowered her head and followed her mother inside. They were quickly seated at a booth complete with vintage vinyl bench seats in a seafoam hue and their own miniature jukebox. Molly took a quick glimpse at the fifties-style décor, which included nostalgic signs advertising malts and banana splits, a red-

and-mustard laminate counter, and a floor covered by tiny black-and-white tiles, and then rounded on her mother.

"What on earth did you say to get us seated?" she demanded suspiciously.

Clara opened her menu and declared, "Baby back ribs! Yum. That's what I'm having." She tossed the menu back on the table and flippantly replied to her daughter's question, "Oh, I just told the charming hostess that you were a reporter and would include a write-up on this establishment in your next piece."

"But this place is already famous. Why would they care if a writer for *Collector's Weekly* wrote about them?"

Clara fidgeted. "Well, I *might* have taken some liberties with the name of your publication."

Molly was appalled. "You didn't say that I wrote for Frommer's again, did you?"

Before Clara could explain, a waitress came by to take their orders. Molly decided on a cheeseburger and a chocolate shake. Charity chose the fried chicken with mashed potatoes and gravy. "You just can't worry about fat or cholesterol when you eat at Ellison's." She sighed. "The last time I was here, I was actually with Tom. We were still married and I wasn't the uptight harpy he thinks . . . he came to think of me as."

Molly thanked the waitress as she delivered a glass of water to her mother, a cherry Coke to Charity, and a frothy milk shake to her. "So your divorce was fairly recent?"

Charity nodded. "Five years ago. I'm not in the antiques business. I'm only at Heart of Dixie as a favor to a friend." She took a sip of soda and looked around. "My, that brings back memories. I love this place, because it's not retro. It's original. They've been running it the same way for something like sixty years and it still works. If only relationships were that permanent." Her expression turned sullen. "Sorry, but it's hard not to be bitter. I never stopped loving Tom, but he was so flighty, so lost in the world of medical antiques, that he became a lousy husband and father. The bad husband part I could have handled, but my kids deserved more."

"Your friend is a dealer showing at Heart of Dixie?" Clara inquired, trying to steer the conversation to a more positive topic.

"Yes. Nell's got the only estate jewelry booth in the show: All That Glitters. I'm a jeweler by trade and Nell and I have been friends since our freshmen year in college, so when her husband got the flu right before they were supposed to leave, I volunteered to help out." She laughed. "Yesterday, I felt like we *were* in college again. We stayed up last night drinking beer and then fell asleep in our room while talking about which male dealers were the best looking."

Molly smiled and then said, "So how did you find out about Tom?"

Charity's grin dissipated. "The police came to our room this morning. They questioned me as to my movements last night as a matter of routine, or at least that's what they said." She offered a wry chuckle. "I hope there isn't anything suspicious about his passing or everyone's sure to blame me. The angry ex-wife always gets blamed." She shrugged with resignation. "I know all of the dealers in the show circuit already think I'm a henpecking harpy, but Tom always owes me money. Right now, he owes for Ashley's braces and for Tom Junior's soccer league. Not to mention his half of the mortgage payment, which is two months behind." She shook her head and sighed, her black tresses shimmering beneath the overhead lights. "Sorry to vent, ladies. I guess I had it good chasing after him with bills that needed paying while he was alive. Now that he's dead, I may have to sell our house. If Tom didn't provide for us in his will, I don't know what'll happen!" She gave Clara a meaningful look. "I would do *anything* to protect my kids' future. I'm sure, as a mother, you understand."

Clara and Molly shifted uncomfortably in their seats as

Charity began to weep, hiding her tears in one of the soda shop's white paper napkins. At this awkward juncture, the waitress arrived with a food-laden tray. Molly's cheeseburger could have fed two professional wrestlers and there were enough spare ribs on Clara's platter to satisfy an entire Little League team. Charity gave one last brush to her eyes and with gusto, dug into her mountain of mashed potatoes drenched in brown gravy. "Now that's comfort food," she mumbled with her mouth full and then chuckled. "I know I shouldn't be hungry at a time like this, but I am."

Molly was startled by the woman's abrupt mood swing. Clara, who was seated next to Charity, licked a bit of barbeque sauce from her finger and said, "I won't hold it against you. At least you're a woman who actually eats."

As they ate, Charity asked the Appleby women about themselves. The threesome made small talk in between bites of succulent food until strains of Elvis's "A Little Less Conversation" rose from the booth next door. Molly examined the songs available on their own jukebox while Clara subtly tried to raise the issue of what would now become of the items in Tom's shop back in Blacksburg, Virginia. But Molly kicked her mother's shin under the table until Clara dropped the topic and focused on stripping the last morsels of meat from her ribs.

Eventually, the conversation between them faltered. Clara cleaned off her hands with a moist toilette and signaled for the check. Glancing surreptitiously at Molly, Clara slid a business card next to Charity's empty plate after she laid down the money to pay for their lunches. "Thanks for introducing us to this delicious soda shop. If we ever come back to Nashville, we'll eat here again. I'd like to try their banana split, but we've got to give formal statements to the police this afternoon," she told Charity. "I hope it doesn't take too long. I'd like to go through Heart of Dixie once more. The dealers always seem to discover brand-new inventories inside their vans and trucks come

Saturday afternoon. It's never the stellar stuff you see on Friday night, but I've bought some wonderful smalls during past shows during that time slot."

Charity glanced at her watch. "I need to make a statement, too. Why don't we all go to the station together and get this over with?" But instead of making an attempt to move, Charity put her face in her hands. "I have to admit," she muttered, "I'm suddenly feeling exhausted. I don't know if it's just that I have a full stomach, but I think the shock is beginning to wear off and I'm realizing that Tom is really gone."

"Let me ask the hostess how to find the station." Molly jumped up, not wanting to witness another round of Charity's weeping. However, the woman remained remarkably composed as they exited the restaurant and she pulled the Lincoln out into traffic and headed south on Twenty-first Avenue. The short drive was spent in silence.

"I appreciate your invitation to lunch," she said as she parked the car a block away from the building housing the police department. "And for listening to me. Not many people would have approached a complete stranger and offered support. Thank you both."

"Well, you've got my card. Call me anytime," Clara replied warmly, grasping Charity's hand.

"Unbelievable," Molly mumbled to herself. Minutes later, the three women approached the receptionist at the front desk.

They had barely explained the purpose of their visit when Detective Butler came striding through a door to the left. Molly was instantly wary of the hard set of his jaw and the angry expression in his eyes. He barked out directions to two fellow officers to take the women to separate rooms.

Molly cast a look of fear at her mother as Clara was led away by a blank-faced policewoman. "Why are we being split up?" she asked the detective. "Has something happened since this morning?"

The detective ignored her as he held open the door to a

small conference room. Another officer waited inside, pressing the buttons on a tape recorder. "I'm not going in there without an answer. What's happened?" Molly repeated her question, her body stiffening as Butler placed a strong palm against the middle of her back and propelled her forward. Reluctantly, she entered the room and took a seat in the chair he pulled out for her.

Seating himself across the table from her, the detective poured himself coffee from a nearby carafe and stirred three packets of sugar into a paper cup. He didn't offer Molly or the second officer any. Instead, he took a deep sip and then, as he replaced the cup on the table, he met Molly's anxious look with a frown. "Something *has* happened since this morning, Miss Appleby." He took another sip of coffee. "A little something called murder."

Chapter 6

"Walking sticks are organic artifacts and must be handled with care. They are quite sensitive to changes in humidity and temperature. Rises in humidity and temperature may lead to swelling and cracking of walking stick shafts and handles."

JEFFREY B. SYNDER, CANES AND WALKING STICKS

"**M**urder?" Molly gasped. "Do you mean Tom...?" The detective ran a meaty hand over the spikes that served as hair in a gesture of annoyance. Molly couldn't tell whether he was irritated by her question or for volunteering such a vital piece of information before her official statement was given.

"State your full name and address please," he commanded briskly after nodding to the second officer. Molly saw the uniformed cop press a button on the recorder before turning her full attention on Detective Butler. Over the next twenty minutes, she offered her account of her movements that morning for the second time. "I can't believe all this happened a few hours ago." She interrupted her narrative. "What a long day." She looked at the clock mounted high on the wall and sighed. "And it's only two."

Butler scowled and silently waved at her with his mechanical pencil to continue. When Molly had recounted all that she could remember, down to the smallest detail such as the names of the tropical plants she had noticed in the garden and the specific hues of Tom's clothes, she leaned back in the uncomfortable metal chair and sighed again.

"And exactly *how* do you know the deceased?" The detective had asked her the exact question that morning, but his tone was much sharper now. As she answered this and a series of other routine queries, Butler routinely clicked the lead up and down in the mechanical pencil until Molly thought she would certainly turn into a murderer if he persisted in repeating the irksome action.

"Can you please stop that?" she finally said in exasperation. "I don't know whether that noise is some kind of interview technique of yours, but I have nothing to hide from you. Mental games are not necessary."

Butler glanced at the pencil as if surprised that it was in his hand and then stuck it inside his suit jacket. "Is there anything else you can add to your statement?"

Molly shook her head. "I'm sorry, but no. I've told you everything I know. Twice. I wish I *could* be of more help. Tom seemed like a very nice man. . . ." She trailed off, thinking of Charity's claim that Tom wasn't the most responsible parent.

The detective seemed to sit upright in his seat all of a sudden. "Has someone indicated that he wasn't *always* such a nice guy?"

Molly was impressed by Butler's shrewdness, but she didn't want to get Charity into hot water. She hesitated and avoided making eye contact.

"We'll find out sooner or later." He glared at Molly. "Let's make it sooner, okay?"

After squirming in her seat for a few seconds, she reluctantly answered. "It was just a few comments that his ex-wife made over lunch. She said that Tom wasn't so good about paying his half of the bills. I'm sure it's a common enough gripe between divorced couples with kids."

Butler exchanged a pointed nod to the other officer and

Molly groaned. She had just provided the Nashville Police Department with their first suspect.

"*If* Tom's been murdered," she said, "it couldn't have been Charity. She was in her hotel room all night and she wasn't alone. She's sharing it with an old college buddy— a dealer named Nell."

Butler raised his eyebrows. "So you're collecting alibis for us, too? Mrs. Barnett's friend could have lied or she could be a heavy sleeper. She might have no idea that Charity snuck out for a few minutes," he argued. At the look of dismay on Molly's face, he softened his tone. "We have to look at every angle. That's why it's important for us to gather *complete* statements."

Molly met his eyes and couldn't help but like the young detective. "I understand and I'd like to offer my assistance. I've actually helped the police out before." She plowed on before Butler could stop her. "Last year, in Richmond, I aided the police in apprehending the Hidden Treasures Killer. That's what the papers dubbed him." She continued self-importantly, "I've got an in with the antiques crowd. I speak their language. And because I'm a reporter, I can ask people questions and they're usually more open with me than they are with the cops. No offense."

"None taken," Butler replied with a hint of amusement.

"And they'll gossip to me, too. Sometimes what people say is nothing but entertaining exaggerations, but every now and then there's a grain of truth in the stories floating around. I know your uncle is Geordie Alexis, but he's a promoter, not a dealer. The dealers aren't going to be as loose-tongued around him as they'd be with me 'cause I'm always on their side. I've proved that in print over and over again. Maybe the little details they'll share with me can help you find your man." She paused, worrying that she had come across as too cocksure. "And I don't think that Charity Barnett is your *man*."

Butler flicked his icy blue gaze at the other officer.

"That's all I need from you, Hank, thanks. Can you check on how things are going with Mrs. Barnett?"

"You got it, Bull," Hank said and left the room.

"Bull?" Molly queried.

"They call me Bull Dog around here. Guess I kind of resemble one with this big, square head and wide shoulders." He gave Molly a severe look. "Plus, I hang on to cases like a pit bull hangs on to a rabbit. My rate of solved cases is the highest in the state." He rubbed his prickly scalp. "Of course, I usually have more time to bag the guilty party. Heart of Dixie closes on Sunday and unless I have a reason to do so, I can hardly ask dozens of dealers to hang out in Nashville so that I can rule them out as suspects one by one."

"Seriously, my mother and I can help you." Molly tried not to make her voice sound too eager. "But first I'll need to know how Tom died."

The detective removed the pencil from his jacket and renewed his agitated clicking. He seemed to be debating over whether to share information with Molly or march her straight to the nearest exit. Finally, he sighed. "This information won't be easy to keep under wraps. Once Uncle Geordie gets wind of what happened, the whole city will find out." More clicking. "My brother did a complete tox screen on Mr. Barnett. Let's just say that a harmful drug was mixed into his margarita. And from what we've learned of his recent behavior, we have no reason to believe this was a suicide. We haven't ruled that out as a possibility, but it's unlikely at this juncture."

Molly immediately thought about the apothecary chests in Tom's booth. Several of the larger chests as well as one or two of the traveling physician's kits used during the Civil War contained dangerous drugs. She shared her thoughts with the detective. He listened closely and occasionally nodded, his eyes betraying a small measure of respect.

"We've examined his inventory and yes, the harmful drug could have come from one of his items, but that doesn't help us much. The questions are, who stole the drugs from one of those chests or canes or whatever, and why?" Detective Butler rose and opened the door. "I see your mama waiting down the hall." He looked down at the case file in his hands. "Thank you for coming in, Miss Appleby. I've got your mobile number and you've got mine. I don't mind you keeping your ears open for me, but be smart about how you handle yourself. Remember, someone inside that show may be a killer."

"I'll be careful," Molly promised and then hurried down the hall to where her mother waited, tapping her large, narrow foot with impatience.

Charity dropped the Applebys off in front of the hotel and drove off to park the car. Once they were inside the mammoth lobby, Clara dragged herself off to see how Darlene was faring while Molly called to check in with Carl.

Digging her cell phone out of her leather tote bag, she decided to call Mark first and update him on the dramatic turn her Nashville assignment had taken. After being nearly swallowed whole by one of the plush armchairs in the lobby, Molly dialed his home number only to reach his answering machine. She then tried his cell, but also received only voice mail. Finally, she called the main number of the *Collector's Weekly* offices.

Though no receptionist would be on duty on a Saturday afternoon, several staff members were likely to be hard at work on the next edition's layout or trying to make article deadlines. During the weekend, the unspoken rule the staff members lived by was to ignore the ringing phone, but if Clayton, the head of the ad department were around, he wouldn't be able to resist answering. Clayton, the self-dubbed "Queen of Classifieds," lived for gossip, and he was a master at gleaning the most intimate information from any number of hapless callers.

Luckily for Molly, Clayton *was* working and after half a dozen rings, he picked up the main line. "Molly, my love!" he crooned into the mouthpiece. "How are things in Dolly Parton Land?"

Knowing that she would make Clayton's day, Molly gave him a quick rundown of how her trip had gone steadily downhill since salesman Al had sat down next to her on the plane on Friday.

"Poor, poor Tom!" Clayton wailed after she told him about the tragic morning. "He was *such* a dear man. So gentle, so easygoing, and he *always* bought half-page ads."

"Maybe he should have stuck with the quarter-page size," Molly commented and then told Clayton about Tom's negligence in regards to giving his ex-wife money.

"I never knew such excitement was to be found at Heart of Dixie." Clayton sighed. "*I* never get to go anywhere. Here I slave, day after day, and am *forced* to live vicariously through you."

"Please, Clayton. You're the epicenter, the very heart of *Collector's Weekly*. The whole paper revolves around you. Why," she teased, "I think it would simply shut down if you ever quit."

"Oh, stop! I can't take the flattery!" he squealed happily. "Now, tell me all about the *gay lords* staying at *Gaylord's* Opryland."

"I'm sure there are a few, but no one is good enough for you, Clayton."

"Thank you, precious, but not to worry! I met a real *prince* last night at the wine bar on Franklin Street."

"Oh?" Molly said, feeling groggy in the soft lap of the expansive chair.

"Ye-es. I overhead him say that he worked for a folk art dealer and so I sashayed a little closer." Clayton paused for effect. "And then I mentioned where *I* worked and he turned to look at me and sweet baby Jesus! He was *so* beautiful—a bronze, black-haired, thirtysomething Alexander the Great who is interested in art and antiques. You know," he trilled, "I think his boss is actually at your show!"

Molly glanced at her watch. It was time to wrap it up with Clayton. "That's great. Are you two going to go out?"

"I guess," Clayton replied with a sulk in his voice. "If I can get past his preference for both guys *and* dolls."

"If anyone can sway the boy, it's you. Now, if you don't mind me changing the subject . . . have you seen Mark around there today?"

"Indeed I have. He has some top secret meeting with Sinister Swanson."

This was news to Molly. "Be a dear and patch me through to his office, would you?"

"Anything for you . . . as long as you promise to call me when there are juicy developments in your latest murder case. Toodles!"

Clayton punched in a few numbers and successfully transferred her to Mark's office line. Molly drummed her fingers against her thigh as it rang, once, twice, and then three times with no answered. She began to grow frustrated. At last, on the fifth ring, Mark picked up rather breathlessly.

"What are you doing at the office today?" Molly asked with more abruptness than she had planned.

"Well hello to you, too," Mark responded huffily in lieu of his usual mixture of calm gentleness. "I was just on my way out the door."

This was not how Molly had intended for their conversation to begin, yet instead of apologizing, she acted like a petulant child. "Look, I've had a pretty tough morning. I could use a kind ear right now *if* you're not too busy."

There was a pause on the other end as if Mark were trying to control his temper. "I never *said* I was too busy." He expelled a loud breath. "What's going on in Nashville?"

Still pouting, Molly almost didn't tell him about Tom, but she found it impossible to keep quiet. After all, Mark couldn't fret over her well-being unless she provided him with a colorful tale about the discovery of the dealer's body. Adding several embellishments, all of which were meant to paint her in a better light, Molly finished talking and awaited Mark's reaction. She never heard it, for Carl Swanson suddenly burst into his office and started raging so loudly in the background that Molly felt as though she were actually in the room.

"You're now officially five minutes *late* for our meeting!" their boss howled at Mark. "Get off that phone and talk to me! I'm not through with *you* yet!"

"Uh . . . I'll call you back later," Mark told Molly hastily and then hung up.

The dial tone blared in her ear until Molly snapped her cell phone shut with annoyance. What was going on back in Durham? Carl didn't usually lose his cool with Mark. Most of the personnel working below Swanson were the recipients of his foul temper, crass remarks, or belittling e-mails, but Carl was completely devoted to the paper and was an excellent editor. Most of his employees often compared him to a circus bear stuck in a cage. He had a fierce growl and could expose an impressive mouthful of fangs, but it was mostly show. At first, Swanson had intimidated Molly, but after two years of working under him, she had grown accustomed to his irascible nature.

"Damn you, Swineson." She grumbled one of his many monikers as she made her way back to the room where Heart of Dixie was being held. "What are you up to?"

Chapter 7

"The President [Franklin Delano Roosevelt] needed a support. It was still an era when a fashionable man wore a cane, and presenting a disabled person with a walking stick was not considered any way a faux pas."

CATHERINE DIKE, CANES IN THE UNITED STATES

If Molly thought her mood was sour, it was nothing compared to that of Howard Rose. He stood to the side of a group of shoppers browsing through the Country Doctor. The New York dealer was shaking his fist at Darlene as she cowered behind a mute and astonished Clara.

"I am going to remove that chest from this booth!" Rose said forcefully as Molly grew close enough to overhear. "It will be on a truck heading to my shop in Manhattan by the time the sun goes down tonight. The piece is rightfully mine!"

"Well, you can't have it," Darlene whimpered. "I heard Mr. Barnett tell you that he had all of the documents necessary to prove that it was *his* to sell."

Rose leaned his powerful body toward Darlene. "And where *are* these 'so-called' documents?" He briefly softened his tone and addressed Clara. She eyed the dealer with a mixture of curiosity and dislike. "Look, I'm sorry Tom is dead, but he couldn't show any papers to me yesterday either. Time's up. The chest comes home with me."

Clara patted Darlene gently on the arm. "Why don't you take a break, dear? That's why I came—to spot you for a bit." She guided the flustered assistant a few feet away from Rose and said, "I'll find out why Mr. Rose believes he has a claim to the chest. Don't worry; I've had a lot of experience dealing with his breed of pompous buffoon. Go get some fresh air or a bite to eat and let me handle him. No man's bullied *me* in decades."

Darlene nodded gratefully and departed, but not before shooting a look of disgust in Howard's direction.

Molly sat in Darlene's folding chair in order to obtain a front row seat for what was undoubtedly going to become the equivalent of a gladiator match. Clara turned her attention back to the arrogant dealer and Rose sized up his opponent in return. He gave the impression that he viewed her as an easily vanquished foe.

"And you are . . . ?" Rose glowered at Clara.

Unruffled, Clara extended an elegant hand. "Clara Appleby. I'm also in the business, but I'm not involved with this show. I'm here solely as a buyer," she added importantly. "However, I work for an auction company and have quite a bit of experience in the legalese of property ownership." She eyed Rose critically. "I assume you have documents in *your* possession alleging that the chest is yours or belongs to one of your clients."

Rose paused, his eyes darting between the painted dower chest in its shadowy corner and his tall and slender female adversary. "This chest most recently belonged to Mr. and Mrs. Chandler McPhee of New Jersey. They bought the chest together, using funds from a joint checking account. Since that time, the McPhees divorced and *Mrs.* McPhee sold the chest without *my* client's permission." Rose continued, his tone laced with irritation, "Mr. McPhee is getting remarried and he wants the chest for his new home. And he will get it, since *he* has the legal right to it."

"So your client, Mr. McPhee, would like to acquire the chest and then have you sell it for a handsome profit, do I have this right?" Clara asked, clearly struggling between a desire to discover all of the facts and wanting to thumb her nose at Rose.

"Your deductions are most astute," Rose replied acidly.

Clara remained unfazed by his unpleasant mannerisms. "Do you have a copy of the couple's divorce settlement?" she asked.

Rose was quickly losing patience with being cross-examined. "I have the bill of sale from when the McPhees purchased the chest. It was *prior* to the divorce. I also have a copy of the cancelled check from their joint account. Mrs. McPhee, who made no significant contributions to said account being that she was a *homemaker*, had no right to sell the chest." His black eyes narrowed. "Much like *you* have no right to interfere in my business."

Clara bristled. "If Tom said he had documentation granting him permission to sell this piece of furniture, then he was telling the truth. Everyone knew what an honest man he was." Clara put her hands on her hips. "I'm sure *Mrs.* Barnett will be most interested in making sure that the chest is sold through the Country Doctor. After all, I'm certain Tom will have bequeathed his business to Charity and their two children. You'll have to take this matter up with her. Luckily," Clara smiled acerbically, "you can find her working in the All That Glitters booth. It's two rows back, near the set of fire doors."

Rose flushed and growled menacingly. "I hardly need another infuriating woman getting in my way! Antiques are truly a man's business. We get things done without all of this useless chitchat. And speaking of *men*—though I use that term loosely in this case—Geordie is an old friend of mine." Rose's expression grew smug. "After the show closes, he'll simply grant me access to this booth and I'll have my way. In fact, I won't be surprised if he hires porters to carry the chest to my van. That redneck fairy can't afford to have me blackball his *precious* show."

Clara refused to allow herself to be baited any further. Instead, she examined her petal-pink nails in a bored fashion. "I made the acquaintance of a rather interesting man today. It so happens he is a detective with the Nashville police. I'm sure he'd be very interested in learning of your heated conversation with Tom yesterday."

Rose barked a dismissive laugh. "Nice try, doll, but I told Butler all about our argument over the chest. He and I had a nice little chat this morning." He laughed again. "I also dropped a few names at the time. See, Governor Robertson and I go way back. He's one of my best clients. In fact, I'm having dinner at the *mansion* tonight, so Butler's not going to give me any trouble. No trouble at all."

"But if you suddenly take off with the chest, you might become a more serious suspect. The police are having a difficult time coming up with a motive. Why would anyone want to kill Tom? Perhaps *someone* needed him out of the way in order to made a profit." Clara walked over to the blanket chest and ran her palm slowly over its lovely surface. "If you steal this piece, which is effectively what you'd be doing, I bet you wouldn't make it a mile down the road."

"No one will stop me." Rose clenched his fists and then released them, smoothing aside a wave of blue-black hair from his perspiring forehead. "Not some hillbilly cop or a gaggle of nosy, insignificant, middle-aged women. Barnett, that no-name, hick dealer is dead and this chest is going to be sitting in the front window of my Fifth Avenue shop by Monday. I would caution *you* not to interfere." To emphasize his point, Rose slapped a broad palm onto the surface of a nearby display glass. Spidery cracks sprang across the surface but the glass did not break. Both Molly and her mother jumped in alarm. "Tell the *widow* Barnett she can bill me for that." Rose gestured at the damaged case and strode off.

"I most certainly will!" Clara retorted lamely and then sank down onto a low stool to the left of the chest. "This piece must be worth more than I thought," she said, staring intensely as the dower chest. "I was thinking somewhere in the neighborhood of fifty thousand dollars but if Howard Rose flew down here to get it, it's got to be a six-figure item."

"I don't like that man." Molly exhaled, feeling as though she had held her breath throughout the entire exchange between Clara and Rose. "What are we going to do?"

"I'm going to tell Charity. We've got to get into Tom's hotel room and find his inventory book. If there *are* any documents we can use against Rose that would make this whole trip worthwhile for me. I've always hated that pompous son-of-a-bitch." She tore her eyes off the chest. "When Rose first started out, he was just another small-time dealer. Then, he inherited a bunch of money from a distant relative and reinvented himself. He changed his name from Hubie Rosenstein to Howard Rose and began to buy up a bunch of prime pieces in order to open his Fifth Avenue store."

"Uh-oh. I'm sensing he outbid you on something," Molly guessed.

"Ironically, it was a miniature painted blanket chest from Berks County, Pennsylvania. Not unlike this one, but with simpler designs that were only on the front. Rose arrived at the auction late—in a stretch limo, if you can believe that—and even though the bidding was over and *everyone* had heard the gavel fall, the lot was reopened. Rose went home with *my* chest. I'll never forgive *him* or that swindling auctioneer for depriving me of that wonderful piece. It was going to form the top tier on my stack of blanket chests in the back bedroom."

"I like the North Carolina miniature in red paint you have there now," Molly offered by way of comfort.

"Thank you, cupcake. Oh, here comes Darlene. You fill her in on that jackass Rose and I'll go talk to Charity. We've got to get inside Tom's room, and pronto."

Molly provided Darlene with a succinct summary of Clara's encounter with Howard Rose. Despite her efforts not to, she found herself yawning repeatedly.

"You poor thing." Darlene looked at her with sympathy. "You've had a long day with a *really* horrible start. And here I've been so worried about myself. How are you holding up?"

Molly covered another yawn with her hand. "I think I'm in need of some caffeine. I'm going to go get a coffee for myself and my mother. Can I get you anything?"

Darlene glanced at her watch. "Well . . . if I have coffee in the afternoon, I'll be up all night. But I doubt I'll be able to sleep anyway, so I'd love a cup. Black with lots of sugar, please."

As Molly headed for the exit, she noticed that the crowds shopping Heart of Dixie had thinned. The show was only open for another hour and the dealers looked either bored or weary as stragglers of disinterested customers fingered their wares while talking on cell phones or attending to shrieking infants in strollers.

Only one more day and the show's over, Molly thought. *And then someone will have gotten away with murder.*

There was a short line at the hotel's cafeteria-style restaurant called Rachel's. Molly looked at the selection of pies and cakes on display with interest. *How can I be hungry after such an enormous lunch*, she wondered and silently fumed at the woman in front of her as she rearranged pieces of chocolate cake in order to get to the largest one.

"Gotta git the best bang for my buck," the woman drawled to the man on her right.

Molly recognized the man's awkward gait and the splint of his right hand. It was Dennis Frazier, the folk art dealer from Chapel Hill. He returned the woman's smile but said nothing as he selected a bag of pretzels and a bottle of water and tucked both items into a bag slung over his left hip. Using his cane for support, he limped over to the cashier and retrieved his wallet from the same bag. Molly was impressed with how well he managed his double handicap.

At last, the woman selected her piece of cake, thumped it down on her tray, and bustled off. Molly returned her attention to the row of white chocolate–raspberry cheesecake slices.

After paying for the three coffees and the cheesecake, Molly decided to eat her treat in the cafeteria for two reasons. The first was that she wanted a moment of peace and quiet in the midst of such a tumultuous day. The second was that she didn't want to listen to Clara's chiding for having such a filling (and fattening) snack when the cocktail and dinner hours were growing near. It only took Molly one bite of delectably creamy cheesecake for her to determine that it was worth it to be less hungry at dinner in order to satisfy her immediate food cravings.

Licking the last dollop of raspberry topping from her fork, Molly stood and arranged the coffees in a takeout tray. She had eaten her cheesecake so quickly that there were still plumes of steam rising out of the cups. As Molly snapped lids onto the cups, she noticed Dennis Frazier seated at a nearby table. He was struggling to open his bag of pretzels. Trying not to stare, Molly watched the dealer hold the bag with his good hand while trying to yank the top open with his teeth. His right hand remained useless within its splint, its fingers curled into a claw. It was hard to observe the dignified man desperately ripping at the snack-sized bag. In the end, his attempts were unsuccessful and he tossed the bag onto the table in frustration.

"Can I give you a hand with that?" Molly asked and

then clamped her fingers over her mouth. "Oops, I'm sorry. I didn't mean to word it that way," she added in embarrassment.

Dennis Frazier smiled. "Don't worry, I'm not that easily offended. I'd be glad for your help, but I think this bag has been sealed shut with Krazy Glue." He handed her the pretzels.

Molly struggled to pull the seams apart but couldn't. Looking around, she grabbed a clean fork from a nearby table and jabbed the tines through the end of the bag. It tore raggedy, ejecting several pretzels onto the table surface in front of Dennis. He laughed. "I've never been assaulted by flying carbohydrates before. Thank you, Miss . . ."

"Molly Appleby." Molly extended her right hand so that Dennis could shake it using his left one. "I was in your booth yesterday. The folk art you've got displayed is wonderful."

Dennis bit into a pretzel, pleased. "Thank you. It has been the passion of my life. I think I live a bit vicariously through those paintings." He pointed at his cane. "Especially the ones that have kids running and playing in them."

Molly recalled seeing Dennis's cane during her brief visit to his booth yesterday. She had believed that his beautiful walking aid had a plain knob for a handle, but she could now see that she had been mistaken in her first impression. What she took for an ivory knob was actually a carved, masculine-looking hand. "Is that a folk art cane?"

"You could say that." Dennis lifted the cane onto the table so that she could have a closer look. "It's a scrimshaw piece, made by a sailor on a whaling ship in the early 1800s."

"Scrimshaw is made from whale bone, right?"

Dennis nodded. "Yes. This cane has a shaft fashioned out of the whale's jawbone. You can't see any of the bone due to these brown strips wound around the entire shaft. Any guess as to what the material is?"

Molly took a seat and leaned over the cane. "I hope it's

not a bull's penis." She laughed. "Someone brought one of those canes into my friend's auction gallery to sell a few months ago. Yours looks a little less petrified—more like a kind of wood."

"It's actually baleen—bones from the inside of a whale's mouth. Sailors embellished scrimshaw canes with it, but to wrap every part but the handle in baleen is unusual."

"May I?" Molly asked before running her hand along the smooth material. She examined the bone handle carved into a closed hand. An object resembling a bird's head poked out from inside the tight fist. The eyes above the long, snoutlike beak seemed to be bulging, as if the force of the hand's curled fingers was suffocating the hapless bird.

Dennis pointed at the bird. "That's an albatross—the bird most feared by seaman in days gone by."

"As in *Rime of the Ancient Mariner*?" Molly tried to remember the eighteenth-century poem. "I haven't read that since freshman year in college, but I know that the mariner killed the albatross and was horribly punished for his deed. The rest of the ship's crew hated him and they all died by the end while he was doomed to live with his remorse." She frowned, perplexed. "With that kind of harsh lesson about animal rights, why would another sailor, one who was almost a contemporary of Coleridge's, carve an albatross being strangled?"

"The seamen also believed that albatrosses were the harbingers of fierce storms as well as the reincarnations of drowned mariners. It *was* thought most unlucky to kill such a bird." Dennis touched the bone beak of the albatross lovingly.

"Then this cane is *really* unusual." Molly stared at it in wonder. "What kind of man would tempt the fates like that? He might have made enemies among his crew just by carving this."

"He would certainly have stood apart among the other

crewmen." Behind his wire-rimmed spectacles, Dennis's gaze grew misty. "Imagine living on that whaling vessel day after day after day. No land in sight. No entertainment but sharing the same old stories or working on pieces of scrimshaw. Could you imagine the boredom, the isolation, the feeling of being trapped on the open water with the same people? People you might not even like, but you can't escape from?"

Molly allowed herself to get caught up in the folk art dealer's vision. "And then, finally, a whale is spotted on the horizon and the hunt begins."

Dennis turned his eyes back to her and smiled warmly. "Yes. Then the men would have felt the life run in their veins again. They would have believed that they had a purpose once more."

"Yet this sailor," Molly gestured at the cane, "must have been pretty unhappy with his chosen profession. This cane is the complete opposite of the lesson from *Ancient Mariner*." She studied the bone bird sadly. "You can almost sense the life draining away from the albatross. Its eyes look . . . tortured."

"I think you're right," Dennis murmured. "The sailor who made this was probably an angry fellow. Angry but patient. It takes a long time to do carving this intricate." He took a drink of water and then remained silent. A glum look had appeared on his face.

Noting the change in Dennis's demeanor, Molly suddenly remembered that the man she was talking to had once been accused of murder. Had she said anything to offend the folk art dealer with her references to the albatross being killed? She hoped not. He seemed like such a gentle, lonely person.

"Well, I'd better get these coffees back before they get any more tepid." She stood. "It was nice talking to you."

Dennis met her eyes and nodded. "And you. It's been a long time since a stranger—particularly such a lovely-looking woman—struck up a conversation with me." He grinned ruefully. "Between my rather infamous history and my physical disabilities, people tend to avoid me. If they do talk to me, they are so overpolite that there's little sincerity in what they say. Mostly, I'm the guy everyone whispers about but no one talks to." He looked down at the cane. "Shows are the worst. This is when I miss my wife the most."

As Molly picked up her carryout tray she struggled to think of something appropriate to say. Then, she was struck with an idea. "I'd like to interview you for *Collector's Weekly* sometime. I write for them, and our offices aren't too far away from your gallery in Chapel Hill. Would you be up for it?"

Dennis hesitated. "My gallery is actually in my house. I have a part-time assistant who handles the minutia of my business. I'm usually on the road doing shows or visiting the artists I buy from. I have one room where I display sale pieces and almost all of my clients visit me by appointment only. So you see, I'm afraid it's not a very interesting setting."

"You could be selling that kind of art tacked onto pieces of cardboard and it would still be fascinating," Molly countered good-humorously. "And I'll bring pretzels."

Dennis issued a brief chuckle. "How can I resist such an offer? Here's my card. I'd be delighted to enlighten anyone about our talented southern folk artists."

Molly slipped his card in her pant pocket and waved goodbye. She had a strong feeling that Dennis was watching her as she walked away. *He's probably thinking that no one else will talk to him for the rest of the show unless they're interested in an item he has for sale. Poor man.*

By the time she returned to the Country Doctor, she had no further opportunities to brood about the folk art dealer. Clara and Charity were standing next to one another, their eyes sweeping the crowd as if looking for someone. Clara looked eager and excited, but the look on Charity's face was darker. There was something hostile and a little bit desperate about the way her eyes raked the room. Molly became a bit flustered when she discovered that she was the person being sought.

"Good Lord, Molly! How long does it take to get coffee?" Clara demanded crossly as Molly placed the tray down in front of Darlene. She barely had time to hand off a cup to Tom's assistant and retrieve the physician's cane she had purchased earlier, now carefully padded in layers of tissue paper and bubble wrap, before Clara was yanking her backward by the arm.

"Come on! Charity's gotten a hold of Tom's room key and we're going to find that inventory book."

"I've got to make sure that chest doesn't go anywhere!" Charity said feverishly. "Your mother told me what it's worth and if Tom owns it outright, then *I'll* own it outright and its sale might just let me keep my house." She rubbed her hands together and her eyes were lit with a spark of maniacal zeal. "I've got to have those documents! I've just got to!" Molly took a step away from her, sensing that she had misjudged Charity as being simply a harmless widow and protective parent. At that moment, Molly saw her in a completely different light. Charity stood like a black panther poised to strike, her face set with determination and anger. If her nails suddenly mutated into four-inch, razor-sharp claws, Molly wouldn't be the least bit surprised.

"Madam! Get a move on," Clara ordered.

Suddenly, Charity smiled, shirking off her darker persona as if she were stepping out of a costume. "Could you come up to Blacksburg and visit?" she teased Clara. "You could really help me get the kids to school on time in the morning."

Clara harrumphed and marched onward.

*   *   *

Tom Barnett's room did not have the balcony overlooking the lush gardens as Molly and Clara's did. The interiors were identical, but his view was of the outside grounds and the soothing white noise of the waterfall did not permeate within.

As with most dealers, Tom had reserved the room for four nights: Thursday, Friday, Saturday, and Sunday. By Monday morning, he had planned to be on the road, heading back to Blacksburg, Virginia. Glancing inside the closet, Molly noted two pairs of pants; one black and one khaki, and two button-downs. One was a crisp white and the second was a buttery yellow with narrow blue pinstripes. A pair of black loafers was lined up beneath the pants and a black belt hung from one of the hangers like a limp asp. In addition to the clothes, Tom had slung a navy windbreaker over one of the pant hangers.

"Do we know what the inventory book looks like?" Molly asked.

Charity, who was examining the zippered compartments of Tom's suitcase, paused in her search. "It's actually a three-ring pocket binder. It's impossible to miss because it's neon orange. Tom bought a few cases of them years ago. He chose that color so that he'd be able to find the book immediately if a client or one of his assistants had a question about one of his items."

"What information did he keep on each item?" Molly queried, opening the small safe inside the closet. It was empty. There was no orange book hidden within the pile of extra pillows or stashed behind the ironing board either.

"Oh, let's say he bought a table from your mom's friend, Lex Lewis," Charity answered. "Tom would keep the receipt from the auction as well as the item's description from the auction catalog. He would mark down the new Country Doctor sale price, the discount he was willing to offer, and how much it eventually sold for. He would also write the date of sale and the method of payment.

Shoot, he practically kept a FBI profile on each customer. Basically, no detail about that table was too small to exclude."

"Must've gone through a lot of orange binders," Clara said, riffling through the drawers beneath the TV cabinet.

"He made a new one every quarter. The old ones are all in boxes at the shop." Charity sighed. "Nothing in the suitcase. I'll check the nightstands."

Molly moved over to the desk. Tom had put nothing personal inside its drawers. The only object that belonged to him was a hardback copy of John Updike's latest novel, *Terrorist*. She headed into the bathroom as Clara and Charity began to peer under the mattresses of the two queen beds.

"Check the toilet tank," Clara ordered.

"Are you serious?" Molly said in disbelief but one look from her mother had her easing back the porcelain lid. "No notebook, Ma, but I found a kilo of cocaine and a wad of hundred-dollar bills stashed inside a Ziploc."

"Very funny," Clara grumbled. "Where else could he have hidden it?"

The three women looked around the room. "We could take the cover off the air vent and look in there," Clara suggested.

Clara frowned. "We'd need a screwdriver."

"Nah. I'll use Tom's toenail clippers," said Charity as she disappeared into the bathroom. When she came back, she was brandishing the grooming tool. "See? There's a nail file on one end."

But the space within the duct lacked any hidden objects. The women exchanged crestfallen looks. "What about his van?" Molly asked.

Charity shook her head. "I've already checked. I have a spare key on my ring in case Tom locked himself out of the van, which he did at least twice a month and usually when he was supposed to be bringing one of the kids somewhere."

"Maybe the police have the binder," Clara wondered

aloud. "After all, they interviewed both Howard Rose and Darlene. They must be aware that the inventory book might prove that Rose was willing to kill for that dower chest."

"No again." Charity sighed. "The police asked *me* if I had the book during today's afternoon grilling session."

"Then there's only one thing left to do," Clara pronounced. "We've got to hide that chest. We can't let Rose take it until we find out where that inventory book is."

"No one's going to help us take it out of the show," Charity argued, deflated. "Who would be willing to cross the high and mighty Howard Rose?"

"Someone equally high and mighty," Clara answered enigmatically. "Come along, madam. It's time to put our feminine wiles to the test."

Chapter 8

"The cane represented and fortified the carrier's personality with a minimum of effort, compared to today's status symbol, the car. The cane was, in poets' words, the exclamation mark of the inner and outer being."

ULRICH KLEVER, WALKINGSTICKS

Clara promised to call Charity once the dower chest had been safely removed and hidden where Howard Rose would never find it.

"How do you plan on keeping that promise?" Molly asked. Once again, she trailed after her mother as Clara headed back toward the antique show with the intentness of hungry cheetah that has just caught a fresh whiff of impala. "And do I have to come along?" Molly whined. "I'm exhausted."

"Just hang in there for a few more minutes, my little turnip green. The show is going to close soon and I need you to distract that redheaded vixen in Grayson Montgomery's booth so that I can put on my damsel in distress act."

"Anyone who knows you would see right through that performance!" Molly spluttered.

"Exactly." Clara lowered her voice. "Grayson is of the rare breed of true, southern gentlemen. I am going to tell him the complete truth and ask for his help. It would go against his code of honor not to lend a hand."

The booth housing Montgomery Antiques & Rare Books was small and incredibly cozy. It had been set up to resemble the reading room of an old manor house. The walls had been papered with forest-green-and-burgundy-striped paper, and an Oriental carpet covered the entire cement floor. The soft light provided by several Tiffany floor lamps highlighted a collection of framed seascapes and a large oil painting of Bryce Canyon in Utah. A piecrust stand held a grouping of bronze statuary that included three hunting dogs and one reclined nude and stood a few feet out from the row of oak barrister's bookcases filled with rare leather-bound tomes that took up the back wall. An inlaid Pembroke table flanked by upholstered wing chairs filled the space to the left while a cherry game table and four Chippendale chairs occupied the area on the right. Grayson and the woman Molly hoped was his assistant sat at the game table, engaged in a game of backgammon.

Other than the two of them, the booth was empty of customers. Grayson and the redhead seemed completely absorbed in their game and did not even look up as Clara and Molly approached.

"Doubles again!" The redhead giggled coquettishly as she moved a red backgammon piece onto a black point in her home quarter. Molly, who had grown up playing backgammon, instantly coveted the hand-painted antique board and wooden dice, but she also took the opportunity to note that neither player wore rings on their left hand.

"You have the luck of a leprechaun," Grayson replied to his opponent with admiration and then slapped his hand on his thigh after his turn with the dice revealed a two and a one; not a good roll if you are racing against your foe to bring your pieces home. "You've escaped me again, my dear," he said, gesturing at the red piece that stood exposed and alone on a black point on Grayson's side of the board. "You had best run while you can."

At that moment, Clara cleared her throat and Grayson looked up from the board, his face breaking into a charming smile. "The lovely Ms. Applebys!" He immediately stood while the redhead scowled and remained seated. "I do hope this is a social call," he said, looking specifically at Clara. "Though you'd be the *most* welcome customer I've greeted all day if indeed, you have come to browse my humble wares."

Clara was clearly affected by Grayson's warmth. "I doubt that your eight-volume series on Confederate generals is anything but humble." She took a step toward Grayson. "Actually, I'm here to beg a favor."

Grayson gave a slight and charming bow. "Anything that is within my power is yours to have." He noted Clara's hesitation to continue and astutely surmised that she wanted to speak with him in private. "Shall we take a stroll? My assistant can handle shutting up for the night should we tarry too long."

Clara took Grayson's proffered arm and Molly couldn't help but notice what a handsome couple the pair made as they wandered off down the aisle between booths. Turning back to the redhead, who was staring after the twosome with a deep frown, Molly introduced herself.

"Yes, I'm aware of your writings," Grayson's assistant, whose name was Belinda Valentine, said dismissively.

Molly was curious about Belinda's role in Grayson's life. Was it purely professional or was there a romantic relationship between the young woman and her wealthy, sophisticated, attractive boss? "So, how long have you been working for Mr. Montgomery?" she asked Belinda, who was resetting the backgammon board.

"Six months," Belinda answered.

"Do you live in Charleston?"

"Yes, but I travel with Mr. Montgomery to *all* of his important events."

Molly removed a book at random from one of the nearby cases and examined it while surreptitiously eyeing Belinda's thick, auburn locks, which fell in soft waves onto a white silk blouse. She noted the other woman's trim waist, small breasts, and incredibly long legs encased in a tight, knee-length suede skirt. Despite her height, Belinda seemed to have been blessed with small, narrow feet, which were elongated by a pair of pumps with a leopard skin pattern. Molly couldn't help but stare at the heels, which were at least three inches high and seemed to be wrapped in shiny patent leather.

"This seems like a fun job," Molly said, hoping to thaw Belinda out enough to coax information from the younger woman, but her attention was suddenly drawn to the price tag of the book she held. "Whoa! Two grand for two books." She looked around the booth and did a quick calculation of how much Grayson's inventory was worth and then turned back to Belinda. "How have sales been?"

Belinda tossed an auburn lock over an elegant shoulder. "We have clients who come to this show solely to purchase wares from us." Molly wasn't sure she cared for the assistant's proprietary tone. "I'm sure you're aware of Mr. Montgomery's reputation for carrying the finest antiquarian books in the south, so this shouldn't be news to you. No pun intended."

"So I guess that means sales have been good." Molly allowed a slight hint of irritation to enter her voice. Why couldn't Belinda just answer her question?

"That book in your hand is one of a two-volume set written by Spenser St. John in the second half of the nineteenth century. It has illustrated folding maps, lithographed plates, and hand-colored botanicals. And look at the pictorial gilt on the spine."

"These look like palm trees to me," Molly observed. As she pivoted the green cloth cover, the light caused the gilt images of exotic-looking foliage to glimmer. She read the title aloud. "*Life in the Forests of the Far East*. Sounds like a botanical travel journal."

Belinda grudgingly agreed. "That would be correct. Spenser studied the Malay language and traveled to Siam, Brunei, and Borneo. He was the private secretary to Sir James Brooke, the British commissioner and governor of Labuan." Another hair toss. "I doubt we'll be packing up this set tomorrow night. These are quite reasonably priced for a first edition in such excellent condition."

Molly carefully returned the book to its niche in one of the oak barrister cases and tried to think of something intelligent to say. She hadn't the foggiest idea where half of the places Belinda just mentioned were, let alone which British explorers had visited them. "I'm impressed," she told Belinda sincerely. "That information wasn't even included on the descriptive card inside the book. Do you know that much about every volume here?"

Belinda smirked ungraciously. "It's called good salesmanship. Mr. Montgomery didn't hire me just for my good looks."

Molly gaped and then flushed. She was guilty of assuming that's exactly why Belinda had been hired.

"It's what everyone always thinks." Belinda glared at Molly, disgusted. "But they're wrong. I have two advanced degrees in literature and history as well as extensive training in the preservation of rare books and maps."

"I was serious when I said I was impressed," Molly said, hoping to soothe Belinda's wounded ego. "I just don't run into many people my age who are interested in antiques, and you're probably even younger than I am."

Grayson's assistant nodded. "I'm the only person working this show with all their original teeth. This room is teeming with octogenarians." She gave Molly a hesitant smile. "I'm sorry to have barked at you or shot you dirty looks. It's just that every other person I deal with comes to the conclusion that I'm some bimbo that Mr. Montgomery keeps around for kicks. I'm so tired of having to prove myself to the blue-blooded, chauvinist clientele we serve." She ran a graceful finger over the tan leather spine of a book called *The History and Geography of the Mississippi Valley.* "Do you run into the same problems or does being a reporter give you more respect than that of a shop girl?"

Molly laughed, feeling a camaraderie blossoming with the sharp-witted redhead. "I doubt you're just a shop girl. I bet you do book restorations, sales, advertising, acquisitions, make travel arrangements, and *still* wake up each morning looking like a cover model. And yes, I've had some negative encounters, but no one's buying anything from me, so I don't *have* to be polite if I don't want to. Most of the people I interview want to tell me their story, whether I'm writing about a collection or an upcoming estate sale, so I guess I'm lucky that way."

"You bet you are! When I'm not dealing with crotchety men I have to waste time pretending to be friendly to a whole troop of divorcées who would do anything to snare Grayson to be their second or third husband." Belinda sat back down at the backgammon table. "And they all come bearing gifts of food; scones, cookies, cakes, breads, muffins, you name it. If Grayson ever gets bored with antiques he can open a bakery."

Molly wondered if Grayson would view Clara as another tiresome divorcée. Somehow she doubted it. "And none of those Sara Lees have gotten to him?"

"Nope." Belinda picked up a pair of dice. "Grayson doesn't really like sweets. Hey, do you play?"

The two women began a new game and exchanged anecdotes about the more lecherous men they had dealt with during their professional careers. By the time Clara and

Grayson returned, Molly felt as though she had made a new friend.

"Thank you again," Clara said by way of goodbye to Grayson.

He stroked his silver beard as his eyes twinkled. "Until this evening then." He smiled and then put a paternal hand on Belinda's shoulder. "Come, my dear. Let's close up shop for the day, shall we?"

"Sounds good to me," Belinda responded. "I can't wait to take off these heels."

Grayson shook his head indulgently at his assistant. "I don't see why you women insist on making yourselves so uncomfortable. We men would treasure you just as much in sensible shoes."

"What a delightful man," Clara whispered happily as she and Molly walked off.

Back in their room, Molly flopped on the bed and closed her eyes. "Mission accomplished, I assume."

"Yes." Clara sat down on the bed and leaned her back against the headboard. She looked fatigued, but oddly radiant.

"What is he going to do with the dower chest?"

Clara shrugged. "Dunno. Grayson said it would be better for me not to know the details so that if anyone asked, I honestly would know nothing about the location of the chest."

"Wow. He *is* a delightful man." Molly opened her eyes and peered at her mother. "And he's doing this just because you asked?"

"Well . . ." Clara colored slightly. "The price for his assistance seemed pretty fair."

"Which was?"

"We have to join him for drinks and dinner." Clara paused, knowing that her daughter would object to the second half of the condition. "And he wanted us to wear our finest."

Molly sat up. "That won't be too fine. We didn't plan on having any fancy dinners while we were here."

Clara sighed. "I know. I told him that. And frankly, I am too pooped to go shopping. He'll just have to take us as we come—in long skirts and sweater sets."

Molly felt weariness washing over her. "You go, Ma. I am way too tired after all that's happened today. For all we know, Tom's murderer is still out there and we've had no luck finding the killer or that damned inventory book. I think I'd rather order room service and go to bed early. We'll have to do a lot more digging tomorrow if we're going to solve either one of these puzzles before the show ends at five."

Clara was about to protest when there was a knock on the door. She got up, opened the door, said "Thank you," and then closed it again. She returned to her bed and placed two large cardboard boxes on the coverlet.

"What are those?" Molly wondered without moving.

"I have no idea," Clara answered and opened the first box. Beneath layers and layers of gold tissue lay some sort of fabric. Clara pulled it out of the box and the deep crimson–colored cloth was revealed as a sheath-styled cocktail dress that was sure to look extremely becoming on Clara. The second box contained a black dress in a light, shimmery fabric with a low neck and an A-line shape; a perfect cut for Molly. Both dresses were the correct size: Clara's was a ten; Molly's, a fourteen.

The note card inside Clara's box read: *Looking forward to our evening. Yours, Grayson Montgomery.*

"I thought things like this only happened in movies." Clara held up her dress and pivoted in front of the closet mirror. "I guess you're going to dinner after all, madam. We can't offend Mr. Montgomery after such a generous gift. You can tell that these dresses weren't cheap. In fact, they probably came from that ritzy boutique in the lobby."

Molly stroked the silky fabric of her dress and sighed.

She sank back against the cloudlike pillows and closed her eyes again. "Wake me up in an hour. That'll give us time to get ready and still stop by that boutique on the way to meet Grayson."

Clara's eyebrows rose. "The boutique? What for?"

Without opening her eyes, Molly gestured at her mother's beloved leather moccasins, which rested in the space between the two beds. "Because we're going to need new shoes."

A dealer named Boyd ran his hand over the inlaid panels of a mahogany Sheraton secretary and then dropped to his knees in order to take a closer look at the feet of the imposing piece.

Carter Chapman, auctioneer and owner of Peachtree Lane, smiled at the familiar sight as one of his best customers switched on the narrow beam of a penlight and inspected the bottom of the bureau. Carter was pleased to see Boyd sit up and reach for his catalog in order to scribble a notation within. Boyd wouldn't be crawling on the floor or writing comments unless he planned to bid on the piece and the North Carolina dealer bid high because his clients were always very wealthy.

"It's a killer piece, wouldn't you say?" he asked Boyd, offering his hand in greeting.

Boyd shook Carter's hand distractedly; his eyes darting back to the fine antique as if he feared it might suddenly disappear. "I like it well enough." He seemed to force himself to relax and finally offered a slight smile. "I've got clients in Baltimore who would like it well enough, too. For the right price, of course."

"Of course." Carter bowed slightly, knowing full well that Boyd would most likely outbid all of Peachtree's other customers in order to secure ownership of the Sheraton bookcase. The idea of a 20 percent commission on a piece sure to capture a winning bid in the five digits made the hardworking auctioneer want to dance a celebratory jig.

"The inlay on that beauty might make my clients happy, but I'm gonna be in the doghouse with my wife if I don't go home with something special for my son's birthday." Boyd looked at Carter in appeal. "He turns eighteen come Monday and I still, for all the world, can't think what to get him."

Carter mused over his customer's predicament, eager to think of another lot in that day's sale he could convince Boyd to bid on. "Now don't I recall you tellin' me that your boy was developin' an interest in primitive art?"

Boyd nodded. "I sure did. He seems to have a real eye for crude carvings and paintings and such. Doesn't matter where it's from either—America, Africa, he likes it all."

"Lemme show you somethin'." Carter led Boyd over to one of the gallery's glass display cases. He produced a ring filled with small brass keys and unlocked one side of the case. Easing open one of the doors, he reached inside the lit recess and removed Lot 119, a wooden cane with a carved cobra head handle.

"Lots of folk artists were partial to symbols, especially snakes. I do believe your son showed a special interest in Garden of Eden themes last time I saw him. I recall he was right fond of pieces with serpents. Now, this is a Continental stick, probably German, but it's as primitive as all can be."

Boyd took the cane from the auctioneer and examined the menacing visage of the cobra. He then scrutinized the *deft carving work that had created the snake's scaled hood. He ran his experienced fingers along the base of the serpent's neck. "Looks like there's some kind of wooden collar here. Is this a system cane?"*

Carter paused for a moment. "Oh! You mean a gadget cane. Sorry, but you know I'm only a simple country auctioneer and don't know all those highfalutin terms. But no, I think that collar is pure decoration. You can see that nothin's disturbed the patina on this beauty since it was made. There'd be cracked glue or somethin' obvious to the eye if that collar had ever been taken off."

"And its provenance?" Boyd asked casually, his eyes riveted on the cane.

Carter grinned. The fish was hooked. "I bought it from the La Fleur family here in Atlanta. Dr. La Fleur had an impressive collection of French furniture that once belonged to his grandfather. He was a doc, too. Lived outside of Paris and bought only the finest stuff. I'm sellin' the bulk of those pieces in my winter sale since all of them are Continental." He gestured at the cane. "Even though this cane isn't American, it seemed to fit in better with this sale than with all that gilt-covered furniture. You Early American dealers wouldn't overlook a primitive piece like this today, but it might get lost in the middle of fifty lots of Sevres porcelain come January."

Boyd flipped through his catalog until he found the description for Lot 119. Carter and his staff had dated the cane as being crafted during the first half of the nineteenth century. "What are the eyes made of?" he asked.

Carter shrugged. "Beats me. I think they're just tiny stones. The wood is ash. A dealer friend of mine said that the black stripes in the bark would have come from a lightnin' strike while the tree was still livin'. Wild, huh?"

"Yes," Boyd agreed, fascinated by the hostility captured in the snake's snarling fangs and lidless white orbs. He put a check mark next to the lot number in his catalog and

thanked Carter. He then bought a coffee from the gallery's snack bar and took his customary seat in the fifth row. A few minutes later, Carter stepped up to the podium, reviewed the terms and conditions of the sale, and began to sell the first lot.

By the time Lot 119 was carried to the front of the room by a comely brunette who pretended to be spooked by the cobra's bared fangs, the rhythm of the auction had been firmly established. Carter paused in his singsong description of the cane long enough to cast an amused glance at his theatrical helper, and then he opened the bidding. Boyd left his number paddle in his lap until the last second, when the bidding seemed to have reached a pinnacle at $250. Just as Carter hesitated before assigning the item as "sold," Boyd flipped his number into the air, catching Carter's sharp eye. In the next few seconds, Boyd fought off a folk art dealer from Birmingham and was able to capture the cane for $325. Satisfied, he sat back in his chair and took a sip of tepid coffee. He had more than fifty lots to wait until the Sheraton secretary would come up for sale.

After asking to borrow the phone in Carter's office, Boyd dialed his home number. When Ellie, his wife of twenty-four years, picked up, Boyd proudly announced that he had found the perfect birthday gift for their son.

"What a relief!" She sounded delighted. "You know, he was talking about becoming an antique dealer over breakfast this morning. I know he's has always enjoyed going to sales with you, but I had no idea he wanted to pursue this as a career. He said that's why he chose Cornell. He wants to get a degree in fine arts and apply for an internship at one of the auction galleries in Manhattan." She paused. "And here I thought he just wanted to be close to that girlfriend of his."

Boyd couldn't have been more pleased. "A dealer! Chip off the ol' block, huh? Well, I'll be home for supper, so pick up a ribbon to tie around the cane and we'll be all set. You buy a cake?"

"Of course not. It's his eighteenth birthday, Boyd. I baked one. A Black Forest with mounds of extra chocolate frosting. Just come on home and you'll see how good it is."

"Hmm, I can almost taste it. See you in a few hours."

After paying a hefty sum for the Sheraton piece on behalf of his clients, Boyd placed the cobra cane on the back seat of his Jaguar sedan and headed north on Interstate 85 toward home. He popped the latest Beatles's album, Revolver, into his eight-track player and sang along with the band to "Tomorrow Never Knows" as he thought about his son.

Enveloped in rosy visions of offering his son a partnership upon his graduation, Boyd drifted lazily along in the right lane, dropping to a few miles below the posted speed limit. The truck driver behind him scowled. He needed to get his load of steel pipes to the construction site in Wilmington before six or he'd receive no bonus. Swerving around the gold Jag, he shot the middle-aged driver a dirty look, but the man behind the wheel was oblivious, his lips moving along with a song.

Boyd was so busy fantasizing about having to order new letterhead for his business to include his son's name that he failed to notice the dangerous appearance of the jiggling pipes on the flatbed passing him. Looking straight ahead, he never saw that one of the heavy ties holding the stack of pipes in place had broken off and was flapping loosely above the right-side pair of rear wheels. The truck barreled ahead of Boyd in a puff of black smoke and a roar of angry acceleration, moving toward a group of orange construction signs warning drivers to expect uneven pavement ahead.

The trucker glanced at his watch and cursed. He barely slowed as he hit the gravelly strip of incomplete asphalt and smiled with pleasure as his front tire took out one of the plastic orange cones lining the shoulder. He turned up his radio and drummed his fingers on the steering wheel in time to "Good Vibrations" by the Beach Boys. He never even noticed the pipes rolling off the back of his flatbed.

Boyd didn't see them either until it was too late. He slammed his brakes as a wave of glinting metal smashed into his windshield, flattening the entire hood, biting deep into the roof of the sedan, and hammering with a powerful force over the surface of the trunk. By the time the Jag skidded violently through a line of orange cones and smacked into the guardrail, it was barely recognizable as a car.

His wife was later informed that Boyd had died almost instantly when the first pipe had penetrated the windshield and struck him full force. She was assured that it was unlikely that her husband had experienced any pain.

Days later, a state trooper arrived at their home with Boyd's personal effects and a long, thin object cocooned in layers of bubble wrap. "Don't know what this is, ma'am," the trooper stated, solemnly handing over the package. "It was on the floor in the back. It's probably broken to bits, but we thought you might want it anyway."

Ellie nodded and accepted the cane. Their son would open it later that night, his eyes blurring with tears. He would fall asleep with the stick in his arms and it would never leave his side as he grew into manhood.

The cane had survived the accident without a scratch.

Chapter 9

"At one time every gentleman 'wore' a cane, just like until most recent days, every man wore a tie . . . And as with ties the more affluent the man, the more canes he had."

FRANCIS H. MONEK, CANES THROUGH THE AGES

When Clara and Molly entered Findley's Irish Pub, a wood-paneled, Victorian-style bar located within the Magnolia area of the hotel, it seemed like the majority of the dealers from Heart of Dixie were already well into their second or third round of drinks.

Grayson and Belinda were seated at one of the wooden tables, protectively guarding two seats as they sipped their cocktails. If Clara was surprised or displeased to see that Belinda would be a part of their evening with Grayson, she gave no sign of either. Upon seeing Clara, Grayson rose gallantly and pulled out a chair for her. The second she was seated, a waiter seemed to appear of out thin air. Grayson ordered Clara's usual, a double Crown Royal with water.

"And for you, miss?" The waiter looked expectantly at Molly.

"What are you having?" Molly asked Belinda.

"The lady's drinking a Nutty Irishman," the waiter answered. His eyes wandered over Belinda's face and then locked on the pale flesh of her cleavage, which was only partially restrained by a gold halter-top. Grayson coughed subtly and the young man blinked and returned his attention to Molly. "It's Bailey's, Frangelico, and Kahlúa with cream. Very tasty, miss."

Molly ordered a Nutty Irishman and then sank deeper into her chair. Across the room, an attractive man in his mid-forties settled himself on a low, three-legged stool and began strumming on his guitar. For a moment, the room grew silent.

"I'm going to sing a few ditties for your pleasure," the entertainer said in a winsome Irish lilt. "If you've got any requests, just write 'em on a dollar bill and put 'em in my pitcher."

He then proceeded to sing a beautifully bittersweet rendition of "I Once Loved A Lass (The False Bride)." Molly felt her eyes misting as she listened to the romantic and mournful lyrics. Looking around the room, most of the female patrons were silently sipping their glasses of beer as they tried to blink back tears, especially after the musician closed his eyes and sang:

> The men in yon forest they are asking me
> How many wild strawberries grow in the salt-sea
> And I answer them back with a tear in my eye
> How many ships sail in the forest.
>
> Go dig me a grave that is long, wide and deep
> And cover it over with flowers so sweet
> That I may lay down there and take a long sleep
> And that's the best way to forget her.

Molly recognized Becky Ross, the textiles dealer. She shared a table with Geordie Alexis. Becky kept rubbing at two marks on her neck that looked suspiciously like hickeys. Having been a teacher, Molly had seen dozens of necks blemished in such a fashion and from the far-off expression in Becky's eyes, Molly was certain that the young quilt dealer had spent an adventurous Friday night in the arms of a man. She was also quite sure that the man was not her tablemate. Geordie was gazing at the singer with utter rapture, his lower lip wobbling as he lost himself in the emotion of the song. Every now and then he would cover his breast with his hand, as if the beauty of the singer and the music were too overwhelming for his heart to withstand.

Charity was there as well, seated at a small table with a plump blonde Molly assumed was Nell, the proprietor of All That Glitters. Tom's ex looked drawn and haggard, her black hair hanging limply over the hand holding her drink. In the farthest corner from the bar, Dennis Frazier sat alone with a pint glass and a plate containing a scattering of French fries, a book open in front of him. Meeting Molly's eyes, he issued a timid smile and raised his glass to her. She smiled back, nodded, and then turned back to the singer.

"Madam." Clara poked Molly's arm. "Write a song down on a five for the poor man. How is he supposed to survive on a few ones?"

"If you can think of a song you'd care to hear," Grayson said, removing a slick leather wallet from an interior pocket of his pearl-gray suit, "I'll write it down for you. This man is a true bard and he deserves more than he's asked us for."

Clara beamed mutely at Grayson, but if the debonair dealer was aware he had scored a big point with the woman seated beside him, he didn't show it.

"I don't know any Irish songs," Molly confessed.

"Oh, I do!" Belinda drained her drink. "Let's have something more lively, or this whole place will be sobbing."

"I agree." Grayson put a hand on top of Clara's. "After what you two ladies have been through today—yes, the grapevine was abuzz by nine A.M. with the news about Tom

Barnett and the details of his demise—it is our duty to make certain that your day ends on a more positive note than it began."

Belinda seemed to be thinking. "I know just the thing! Write down 'Whiskey in the Jar.'"

Grayson wrote down the title and Belinda took the c-note up to the singer's pitcher. When the musician saw the bill's denomination and the lovely vision delivering it, he practically snapped a guitar string. After reading the requested song title, the performer insisted Belinda sit in front of him so that he could properly serenade her.

As the song commenced, Clara leaned toward Grayson and began to fill him in on their lunch with Charity, the interviews at the police station, and their failure to find the inventory book. Grayson listened carefully and never interrupted. For once, Molly didn't have the energy to chime in or correct small errors in Clara's narrative. With Belinda's disappearance, Molly was feeling a bit like the third wheel. Finally, Clara came to the end of their tale when Grayson's dark blue eyes suddenly flew open wide.

"Wait a moment!" he exclaimed though Molly could barely hear him over the crowd, who had begun to clap in time with the musician's jovial song. It was apparently a popular ditty as half of the audience members, including Belinda, joined in to sing the chorus:

> With me ring dum a doodle um dah
> Whack for the daddy
> Whack for the daddy
> There's whiskey in the jar

Molly had to strain her ears over the shouting crooners, but Grayson seemed to be gathering his thoughts. Finally, he raised his voice slightly so that it carried across the table to where Molly sat. "I overheard a snippet of conversation between Tom and Cornelius Leitts on Friday night that might help solve the mystery of the missing book."

"You wonderful man, you." Clara gushed. Her upper body was so close to Grayson's that she was practically sitting in his lap. As if suddenly aware of the eagerness she was illustrating, Clara sat back, ramrod straight in her chair, but gave Grayson's hand a little squeeze of encouragement. "Tell us everything!" she ordered, sounding more like her old self. Molly wasn't sure if she could grow accustomed to Clara ogling Grayson like an enamored teenager drooling over the lead singer from the latest boy band.

"You must know Cornelius, Clara. He's been doing this show for years." Grayson subtly lifted his index finger in the direction of the bar. "That's the man, sitting on the bar stool closest to our Irish singer."

Clara swiveled her head and then frowned in confusion. "The man in the white turtleneck with the checked jacket?"

"Yes," Grayson answered.

"I thought his name was Cotton."

Grayson chuckled. "That is his nickname, yes."

Molly observed the older man at the bar. He had a round, wrinkled face, wide and liquid-looking dark brown eyes, a thick neck, and the biggest ears Molly had ever seen. Tufts of white hair protruded from within the enormous external organs while feathers of silver and white hair stuck out at impossible angles on both sides of Cotton's head.

"He looks like a koala bear," Molly remarked unpleasantly as she reached for her glass, only to find it empty. Her stomach grumbled with hunger and the raucous Irish song was beginning to grate on her frayed nerves. She wished Grayson would make his point and then immediately regretted her negative feelings. It wasn't Grayson's fault that she was so tired.

"He does resemble that marsupial, as a matter of fact, but Cotton is one of Tom's oldest friends. In fact, Tom used to work for Cotton when the older gentleman still had a shop in Blacksburg. He now operates solely from Charlottesville, I believe."

"And his connection to the book?" Clara asked, raising a pair of impatient eyebrows.

"My apologies, fair lady. On Friday evening, I happened to be talking shop with Belinda in the Jack Daniel's Saloon, the bar located in the Garden section of this luxurious compound. Being that most of the other dealers were on their way to the preview party, the bar was fairly empty. I don't particularly enjoy margaritas, so Belinda reluctantly agreed to keep me company so that I might enjoy a glass of Old No. 7." He paused, grinned at Clara's exasperated expression, and took a slow, satisfying sip of what Molly assumed was straight whiskey. "Tom and Cotton were talking at the bar. Actually, Tom was talking, in quite an agitated manner, and Cotton was listening. I don't normally eavesdrop on conversations, but Belinda had gone off to powder her nose and I was just sitting there pondering over a business venture I will tell you about at a more appropriate time, so I heard a portion of what Tom said."

Clara had returned to the edge of her seat. Her glass was also empty. "Did he mention the inventory book?"

"The three phrases I heard Tom say to Cotton were '*Now I know how he got away with it,*' and '*The proof is in this book,*' and '*I'm afraid he saw me.*'" Grayson shrugged. "None of that makes much sense to me, except for the mention of the book."

"Tom must have given Cotton the book!" Clara exclaimed. "He obviously had it with him because he said '*this* book.'"

"I think you're right, Ma," Molly agreed. "Tom was clearly scared of having the book fall into the wrong hands. The 'he' must be Howard Rose."

Clara snorted. "Rose certainly seems capable of murder."

Grayson rubbed his neat, silver beard. "It is true that Howard is an impolite person and doesn't seem to enjoy the success he has worked so hard to obtain, but I don't think we can quickly conclude that he put an end to Tom's life."

"Let's get back to the book," Molly said. "I'd bet my collection of southern pottery that Cotton has it in his possession." She stood.

"Where are you going?" Clara inquired.

"To talk to the human koala bear. I'm going to mention the book and see how he reacts."

Clara shook her glass so that the melting ice rattled. "Good idea. And while you're up, gumdrop . . ."

"Yes, yes." Molly sighed theatrically. "I'll send a waiter back to the table."

"Whiskey in a Jar" had finally come to a conclusion and Belinda rose, accepted a kiss on the cheek from the singer, and rejoined Clara and Grayson. Molly saw that a stool had opened up alongside Cotton and she hastily planted her bottom on it before anyone else had the chance. She ordered another Nutty Irishman and asked the bartender to send a server to where Clara sat looking forlornly at the ice in her glass. At that moment, Clara raised her eyes and looked at Molly expectantly. Molly wasn't sure if her mother was more interested in her nip or in her daughter's ability to extract personal and potentially dangerous information from a complete stranger.

Molly began with a polite hello, which Cotton returned. Then, just as she was about to introduce herself, Cotton began patting the pocket of his suit jacket as if a large insect was trapped inside. Wearing a surprised expression, he withdrew a cell phone, which had clearly been set to vibrate. He looked at the phone as though he had no idea what to do with it and then awkwardly flipped it open and held it helplessly in his hand.

"YOUR EAR, COTTON!" a voice on the other end screamed. "PUT THE PHONE UP TO YOUR EAR!"

Molly was positive that the entire bar could have heard and followed the shouted directions, but Cotton was not quick to react. He moved the phone toward his gigantic right ear in a sloth-like motion and then whispered, "Yes? Hello? Is that you Esther?"

"OF COURSE! CAN YOU HEAR ME?"

"Yes, dear. You know I haven't got the hang of these mobile phones." Cotton flicked his eyes toward Molly and then pivoted his shoulder slightly, as if indicating that he'd like some privacy. Molly turned away and took out her own cell phone from her purse. She made a big show of pretending to dial a number and then held it up to her ear and began to nod and grunt as if she were listening to an incredibly interesting anecdote. Her ruse seemed to work, but just as Cotton began to talk to Esther, who Molly assumed was his wife, the Irish performer began to sing "Danny Boy" and it seemed like everyone in Nashville was joining in.

"I said I'm managing, but barely!" Cotton had to talk louder in order to hear his own voice over the music. "Yes, I'm in a bar! Well . . . it's been a long day! Didn't you get my message about Tom Barnett?"

There was a long pause. Molly began to laugh as though she had just heard the best joke in the world. "You are too much, Kitty!" she squealed, using her best friend's name out of habit.

"No, I didn't tell the police," Cotton resumed speaking, but he lowered his voice so much that if Molly hadn't had what she called 'teacher hearing,' his next sentence would have been lost to her. "Because I promised Tom to keep the book. And now he's dead, Esther! Murdered! *I* could be next!" A pause. "It's hidden in our favorite piece. . . . What do you *mean* you're on your way? When? That's not a good idea, sweetheart. . . . Yes, I'll see you in the morning. Yes, dear, I'm wearing it right now. . . . Okay, I'm going back to my room now. See you soon."

Molly heard the phone click shut and turned back toward the bar. She pretended to continue with her conversation as Cotton placed a ten-dollar bill next to his empty mug and nodded stiffly to the bartender. It was then that Molly noticed that Cotton was wearing some kind of neck brace. It wasn't visible above the turtleneck, but its rigid outlines could be seen through the shirt's thin white fabric.

What happened to him? Molly wondered as she watched Cotton leave the bar. *The antique business seems to grow more dangerous every year!*

Back at their table, Grayson was paying the tab while Clara polished off the remnants of her second cocktail. Belinda was nowhere to be seen.

"Where did Belinda go?" Molly asked as she rejoined the group.

Clara gestured at the musician. "They're going to have dinner during his break. She went to change into something more casual. Did you find out anything?"

Molly sank down into a seat. "Cotton has the inventory book. I'm sure of it."

"Really?" Clara breathed. "You'll have to wait to tell us during dinner. It's too loud in here and I'm hungry enough to eat the biggest steak on the menu."

Grayson held out Clara's chair. "Now that's the kind of dining companion a man likes to have. Shall we?"

Molly didn't think she could remain vertical for another second. "You two go ahead without me. I'm going to order some potato soup and a salad and go lie down." She held up a hand to stop her mother's protests. "Really, Ma. I've had it. Mr. Montgomery, thank you for the invitation and for the lovely dress as well."

Clara touched Molly's cheek with concern. "Are you sure, honey?"

"I'm sure. Cotton is going back to his room, too. It

sounds like his wife is coming here in the morning. I'll get up early and pay him a visit before she arrives and simply ask to see the inventory book. If he won't show me, he'll show Detective Butler." Molly rubbed at her tired eyes. "Whatever secret is in there can keep until then."

"I hope so." Clara gave her daughter a quick hug and then strolled away with Grayson.

Molly watched them go. She felt a pang of loneliness and regretted her attitude during her short conversation with Mark. She decided to call him and apologize, but after changing into pajamas and filling her stomach with warm and creamy potato soup, sprinkled with cheese, chives, and bacon bits, she fell asleep with the television and all of the lights on. She didn't even hear her mother return from her date with Grayson.

Clara turned off the lights and pulled a blanket over Molly's inert form. Her daughter was talking in her sleep; her lips moved rapidly and indiscernible words tumbled out. It was well after midnight before the room finally grew completely quiet, but neither woman slept soundly. Both of their dreams were plagued by images of orange notebooks, dower chests resting in the shadows, intimidating policemen, and a body nestled among a cluster of heady and exotic plants.

Chapter 10

*"European aristocracy of the seventeenth and eighteenth century,
concerned that the common folk would rise against them or brig-
ands would assault them, were among the first to order walking
sticks with swords and daggers hidden within their shafts. Considering everyone was armed during this period, the fear seems
reasonable."*

JEFFREY B. SNYDER, CANES AND WALKING STICKS

M olly had been planning on sleeping late. On Sunday, Heart of Dixie didn't open its doors until ten
and most of the dealers expected a slow morning, being
that the majority of the family-type shoppers who would
frequent the show were likely to attend worship service
first. Things wouldn't pick up until after 1 P.M., when most
of the customers had gone to church followed by the customary meal at one of the local buffet restaurants proudly
serving piles of gravy-drenched roast, starchy vegetables,
buttered rolls, and a bounty of desserts to its pious patrons.
Molly attended church when she was home in Durham, but
had no inclination to seek out the nearest Methodist church
in Nashville. When she traveled, she preferred to spend Sunday mornings in a more hedonistic manner—drinking coffee, eating carb-loaded croissants or sugary pastries, and
sleeping late. On this morning, however, there would be little opportunity for lounging in bed.

"Is someone knocking?" Clara's voice penetrated the stillness of the darkened room.

Molly tried to swim to the surface of wakefulness and was helped along by the sound of polite, yet determined rapping on their hotel room door. Slipping her feet into her flip-flops, she shuffled to the door and peered out the keyhole. Wiley, the cute bellhop who looked prepared to ditch his job at any moment in order to hit the waves, stood on the opposite side, bearing a tray containing a carafe of coffee, two cups and saucers, and a silver-plated vase filled with a sprig of purple emperor sedum.

"Good morning!" Wiley beamed. "I'm on dawn patrol today and I've got some fresh joe for ya. Compliments of the house. I hear your in-room coffeemaker went carrots yesterday. Bummer, huh?"

Molly wondered if she were still asleep. Wiley wasn't making any sense. "Carrots?" she asked. The tantalizing aroma emanating from the coffee tray convinced her she was not.

"Oh, it's surfer lingo. Means to get wiped out." Wiley looked Molly up and down, smiling as he took in the sight of her pajamas, which were powder blue and covered with designs of perky, bright red cherries. "You know, like, by a wave?"

"Gotcha." Molly took the tray from Wiley's hands, struggled to place the unwieldy item on the desk, and took the folded dollar bills Clara held out to her. She returned to the threshold and handed Wiley his tip. He flipped his white-blond hair out of his eyes as he accepted the money and then hesitated.

"So . . ." he began.

Molly looked at her watch. It was quarter after seven. Way too early to attempt any kind of civil conversation. "Okay, Wiley. Gotta run. Thanks again for the coffee," she said, shutting the door on him.

Clara had donned a tattered and well-loved cotton robe

over her nightshirt and was already pouring the coffee. "'We apologize for yesterday's inconvenience,'" she read from the typed note card propped upon the tray. "How nice. Let's have our coffee out on the balcony."

"Hmm." Molly closed her eyes and inhaled the heavenly scent. "It smells like hazelnut." She poured herself a cup, added an artificial sweetener, mixed in liberal amounts of cream, and got comfortable on one of the chairs on the balcony. She listened to the soothing pulse of the waterfall and sighed as she sipped the fresh, hot brew. The coffee was delicious, but Molly felt as though she could easily return to bed and immediately fall back to sleep.

"You were tossing and turning last night like a fish on the line." Clara eyed her daughter over the rim of her cup. "I didn't sleep too well either." She frowned. "Here we are, enjoying free coffee on our balcony while Tom is gone, Charity has to deal with funeral arrangements and bills and lawyers, Darlene is on the verge of mental collapse, and *we* haven't found any proof to use in fending off Howard Rose." She fiddled with her teaspoon, absently stirring it around and around in her half-filled cup. "We're going to have to turn that dower chest over to him if we don't get our hands on that inventory book."

"I'm going to visit Cotton's room as soon as I get dressed," Molly assured her mother. "He's got the book and hopefully, answers to all the riddles are inside."

"Well, you'd better get going. Cotton's no spring chicken and you know how old people are early risers. Just think of your grandmother. She's probably eating lunch right about now."

Molly took a final swallow of coffee and headed for the bathroom. As she was about to turn the shower on, there was another knock on their door. This time, Clara opened it.

"More coffee!" she exclaimed. Molly joined her by the doorway. Another tray had been placed outside their door, but the delivery person had already departed. Molly retrieved the heavy lacquer tray and brought it inside.

"They must have filled our complimentary order twice," Clara suggested, brandishing another note card. "Only difference is that this one's handwritten."

Molly took the note from Clara's hand. "And the paper's not the same. It's not as thick as the first card." She held the two cards side by side and then opened the top drawer of their desk. A selection of stationary rested within, including several note cards. The note on their second tray of free coffee had been written using such a card, but the first had not.

"I can't drink more than two cups right now anyway." Clara waved a dismissive hand at the tray. "Why are you making that face?"

Molly realized she was chewing on her bottom lip as she glared at the two cards. "Well, this second note is on the same paper we all have in our rooms and just reads 'Compliments of the house.' It seems a little odd to me." She unscrewed the lid to the carafe and gave the steaming liquid a good whiff.

"Does it smell like almonds, Ms. Christie?" her mother teased. "A little cyanide first thing in the morning?"

"Hazelnut," Molly replied with a scowl. She then determinedly picked up the phone and dialed the extension for room service. She explained the mixup and asked who had delivered the second tray, as she had had no opportunity to give the speedy employee a tip.

"We only brought one service to your room, ma'am," the room service manager said. "Wiley took it upstairs at five after seven. There must be some mistake about the second delivery. I'm sorry to have disturbed your morning. Just leave it outside the door and I'll send someone to collect it immediately."

"Oh, it's not in our way at all!" Molly gushed. "We may

even drink it since it's here. Thank you for your time." She hung up.

"They didn't send this tray?" Clara asked, her curiosity piqued.

Molly shrugged. "They have no record of doing so. Don't drink any of that, Ma. I'm serious. Someone might have guessed that we're conducting our own little investigation into Tom's murder and they might not approve." Briskly, she examined the note card one more time and then dropped it onto the tray. "I'm hitting the shower."

Five minutes later, Clara was knocking on the closed bathroom door. "Hurry it up, madam. I just called Cotton's room and there's no answer. That means we've got to find him wherever he's having breakfast. You can shave your legs when you're back in Durham."

Molly looked down at the streak of exposed skin on her left leg. She had just finished slathering her entire limb with shaving cream. How had her mother known?

Clara showered as Molly partially dried her thick hair. Forgoing any makeup except for mascara and lipstick, she was ready and waiting while her mother finished brushing her hair.

In the elevator, Molly hummed along with "Greensleeves." She felt refreshed and hopeful. All they had to do was locate Cotton within one of the hotel's eateries. Molly doubted he would leave the immediate vicinity considering his wife was on her way. The elevator paused on the third floor and two young police officers in neat blue uniforms stepped on. Their grim faces and muteness instantly raised the hairs on Molly's neck.

"Excuse me," she said to the female officer, who looked as though she was fresh out of high school. "Has something happened? Is everything okay?"

The officer, whose last name was Reed according to the shiny badge pinned to her breast pocket, kept her expression completely blank as she answered, "Nothing to worry about, ma'am." She then tacked on a weak smile, which never reached her eyes. The second officer was boyish-looking and skinny. He cast his eyes to the ground and studied the elevator carpet with intense interest. Molly was now positive that Officer Reed was lying when she claimed that there was nothing to worry about.

"Detective Butler wouldn't be here in the hotel right now, would he?" Molly persisted.

The two officers exchanged surprised looks. "Why do you ask?" Reed inquired brusquely, her hand shooting out in order to hold the elevators doors open.

Molly drew herself up. "I have some information to share with him regarding the death of Tom Barnett," she declared importantly.

"You do?" Clara squeaked and was quickly elbowed in the ribs by her daughter.

Officer Reed hesitated, then removed her walkie-talkie from her belt and called for the detective. She asked Molly who she was and what information she had to impart. Molly gave her name and then insisted that she needed to tell Butler the information in person. Reed looked disgusted but transmitted the message to Butler, indicating that Molly and Clara should step out of the elevator. She then jerked her thumb toward the third-floor stairwell door. "We'll wait for him here."

"What did you do that for?" Clara hissed as the elevator doors closed and all four were awaiting the arrival of Detective Butler. "Now we can't look for Cotton."

"We will, just not this second. What if someone else has been killed?" Molly whispered back a bit frantically. "If the killer had been caught, why would these two act so bothered?"

Clara shook her head and cast a sidelong glance at the officers. Reed was biting the nail on her pinky finger and the young male officer was shining the surface of his watch using his shirtcuff. Clara's voice was filled with doubt. "Why assume someone was hurt? Butler could be here interviewing dealers about Tom. These two could just be bored."

"At least three cops are here in the hotel at seven-thirty in the morning?" Molly shook her head. "No way is this an interview. The killer is still out there, and as soon as I saw the look on the faces of these two . . ." She dropped her voice and discreetly gestured at the two cops. "I've seen that look before, Ma. It's how people act when they've seen something shocking. I saw it on a dozen faces in Richmond when those poor people got an eyeful of that woman appraiser hung with her own scarf. Officer Reed over there has seen something she's never seen before. You can tell by watching her eyes."

"Harrumph," Clara snorted. "I didn't realize you were an expert in physiognomy." She crossed her arms over her chest and tapped her foot with impatience. "Uh-oh. Here comes Butler and he doesn't look overjoyed to see us."

Detective Butler approached like a locomotive traveling at full steam. His eyes were narrowed and his neck was tucked into his massive shoulders as he strutted down the hall in an unfaltering gait that was both hurried and menacing. Molly flinched and Clara drew a deep breath as if preparing for impact.

"No wonder they call him Bulldog," Molly whimpered. "I feel like he's about to tear out my throat and leave me for dead."

Butler came to a sudden halt inches from Molly's face. "I hope you have a good reason for needing to speak to me," he growled. "I'm rather busy at the moment."

Molly knew it was unwise to provoke the already agitated detective, but she couldn't help herself. "What's happened?"

Ignoring her question, Butler waved at the Appleby women to move farther away from the elevators as they disgorged a loud group of men wearing camo jackets and baseball caps bearing name brands like Stihl, Columbia Sportswear, and the Tractor Supply Company.

"I'm gonna win the Gobbling competition this year," one of the men boasted happily as he tipped his cap at the Applebys. "Y'all can just congratulate me right now. I've been practicin' every day since last year. Wanna hear?"

"No!" the rest of his assembly answered in unison.

"Save it for the stage, Buddy." An unshaven man chewing on a straw eyed the two police officers. He stopped in front of Butler and said, "These two purty ladies aren't in no kind of trouble, are they?"

"Not at all, sir," Butler replied woodenly. "We're just having a friendly chat."

"Sure, sure." The man nodded at his fellows. "We've all had a few 'chats' with the law, too." The men laughed. "You girlies come get us if you need bail money, ya hear? We're down the hall in 344. Just listen for the turkey call." Guffawing, they moved away and Butler turned his attention back to Molly.

"So? You have some information for me?" His blue eyes were steely, his stance impatient and authoritative. Molly felt her resolve to uncover what brought Butler back to the hotel quickly evaporating.

Quietly, she described the claim made by Howard Rose regarding the dower chest and the likelihood that Cotton was in possession of Tom Barnett's missing inventory book. "You see," Molly said, warming up to her tale, "the book *must* contain some clue as to who killed Tom. *I* suspect that Rose is a likely candidate. He could make a fortune selling that dower chest and it would only increase his reputation within the antique world."

Butler rubbed the bristles on his scalp and consulted his copy of the Heart of Dixie show brochure. "Who is Cotton? If he's a dealer, he isn't listed in here."

Clara stepped forward. "She's referring to Cornelius

Leitts. His nickname is Cotton." She pointed at the map of dealer booths. "Here's his booth, in the front left corner of the room."

Something flashed in Butler's eyes. "And you believe Cotton has Tom Barnett's inventory book hidden somewhere in his booth."

Molly refused to divulge the last and most significant piece of information. "Yes. That's the impression I got when I heard him talking to his wife."

"Why not in his room or in his truck?" Butler persisted. "What *exactly* did he say to give you that impression?" His eyes bored into her.

"Um . . ." Molly pretended as though she were trying to remember.

"He said it was hidden in a piece," Clara answered and then immediately added, despite receiving sullen looks from her daughter, "as in a secret compartment. That could only refer to a piece in his booth."

"Thank you," Butler said to Clara as Molly longed to throttle her mother. "We'll get right on that. As soon as I get a hold of Mrs. Leitts."

"Mrs.?" Molly stared at Butler, momentarily forgetting that Clara had ruined their best chance of beating out all other parties to the inventory book. "Why not just ask Cotton?"

Butler said nothing, but once again the two young officers exchanged worried glances.

"He is unable to communicate at this time," Butler offered by way of reply.

"Is that code for he's dead?" Molly was suddenly angry with herself. "Last night he was a frightened old man in a bar. Oh God; if I had only called you right after I heard him on the phone he might still be alive!" She turned toward her mother. "I was just so tired." Her eyes filled with tears. "I wanted to be the one to solve this murder. Look what my selfishness has caused."

Butler clamped a hand on her arm. "Wait a minute here! Cotton's not dead!" He lowered his voice. "Someone *tried* to kill him. He was stabbed in the neck but managed to call for help in time. He's in the hospital in stable condition."

Molly covered her mouth as she pictured a gaping wound in Cotton's neck. She could imagine the blood gurgling from his jugular like water bubbling in a fast-flowing stream as he clutched his throat in an effort to staunch the life-ending flow. How did someone survive a dire wound like that? "The neck brace!" she exclaimed with relief. "Is that what saved him?"

Butler nodded.

"Thank the Lord!" Molly rubbed her forehead as she continued to grapple with the alarming news. "But that proves my theory! Someone is desperate for that inventory book. In fact, the killer may have already found it! You'd better check out Rose's room. If the book's not there, then it's still safely hidden in Cotton's booth."

"We'll get on it right away," was Butler's mocking reply. "Now if you'll both—" the detective began his dismissal of the Appleby women.

"How?" Clara interrupted forcefully. "You can't just pull apart antique pieces of furniture with hammer and screwdriver. You'll need someone who is an expert at finding which piece could house the book and how to operate the release mechanism, if there is one." She paused. "Is Cotton able to communicate?"

Butler rubbed his head again. "He can't speak due to the location of the wound and he's heavily sedated as well. He's suffering from shock, but when he wakes up we'll have him write where he hid the book on a piece of paper . . . if we don't find it ourselves first," he added with confidence.

"Your department could get sued for damages, you know," Clara pointed out. Molly was afraid that her mother had gone too far. "You could wait until Cotton wakes up or

Mrs. Leitts arrives while the killer is hundreds of miles away, drinking cocktails on some beach. Or *we* could help you . . ." She raised her voice suggestively.

"You're an expert when it comes to secrets, I'm sure," Butler said flatly. "Thank you, but my team will handle this situation from here on out. If we are unsuccessful in Cotton's booth I'll enlist my uncle Geordie to aid us. Now please! I have many things to do and I'm running short on time."

Butler abruptly shook their hands and then disappeared into the stairwell. Suddenly remembering the suspicious coffee carafe, Molly ducked in after him. She called his name, but Butler had either sprinted down to the lobby or made a decision to ignore her yelling. Fuming, Molly raced down the stairs after him, growing more irritated by the realization that going down stairs was becoming almost as exerting as going up.

"I'm starting a diet when this trip is over," Molly vowed to herself.

The lobby was crowded with visitors checking out, reading newspapers while sipping coffee, or milling about near the automatic doors as they waited to be led to a tour bus. Molly spotted Butler leaning against a wall behind an enormous potted fern. He had a cell phone sandwiched between his ear and his shoulder and was scribbling notes on a small pad. Molly squatted on the other side of the fern.

"You know the cause of death for Barnett?" she heard him say. "Hm. Never heard of that. What exactly is it, bro?" He listened for almost a full minute as Molly shifted nervously on her cramping legs. "Opium, huh?" Butler rubbed his head and then flipped his notebook open and made a few quick notations. "Ipecac and what? Got it. I seem to remember a bunch of old drugs in Tom's booth but I don't know if all three of those were in those boxes or glass jars the docs used in the old days. I'll check it out, thanks."

Molly froze as Butler flipped his notebook closed. "I'd better run. I've got two booths to search before the show opens. Uncle Geordie is already throwing a fit over Cornelius Leitts's accident." He paused. "You know Geordie. He's going to man Leitts's booth himself . . . at least until Mrs. Leitts appears." He sighed. "Too many suspects for my taste. Anyone could have stolen drugs from Tom's booth. Yeah, thanks. I need a little luck right now."

As Butler hung up and shoved the phone into his front pocket, Molly jumped into one of the oversized chairs whose back faced Butler and grabbed a stray magazine. Hiding her face, she felt like some inept spy. Seconds later, she peered over the copy of *AARP* magazine featuring a smirking William Shatner on the cover, and noticed Clara searching around the lobby for her. Molly got up and waved her over.

"Is it too early to start drinking?" she asked her mother.

Her mother shrugged. "For me it is, but I suppose you could get a mimosa from one of the restaurants. Why?"

"Tom was poisoned with opium. It probably came from his own booth."

Clara's gray eyes widened. "From one of the apothecary boxes!"

"Or my physician's cane!" Molly hissed. "It had an unopened vial of morphine pills hidden inside."

"Who would bother with a cane when there were little bottles of pills readily available in the apothecary boxes? It would have been much more obvious if someone stood around removing vials from that cane." Clara placed her hands over her flat stomach. "Now that we don't have to rush to Cotton's room, let's get something to eat."

Molly was about to lecture her mother on her callousness when her own stomach rumbled like distant thunder. Over plates of eggs Benedict loaded with Hollandaise sauce, buttered rye toast, and bowls of fresh fruit salad garnished with mint leaves, Clara suddenly began to snicker.

"What's so funny?" Molly asked crabbily. Thus far, the morning had not progressed very pleasantly.

"Oh, I know you're cross because that detective didn't appreciate your contributions to his case, but I'm sure he'll need our help before the morning is out." She took a sip of fresh-squeezed orange juice. "Geordie is a show promoter. He's a salesman who happens to produce some very successful shows. What he is not, is an expert on antique furniture. By the time we go back to the room, brush our teeth, and return to the show, that detective will be begging for us to help him find that inventory book."

Molly frowned. "Begging? Somehow I doubt it."

Clara wiped her lips with her napkin and leaned forward on her elbows. "You seem abnormally irritable today." She raised an elegant eyebrow. "Are you quarreling with Mark?"

Molly fidgeted with her water glass. "You are!" Clara looked disappointed. "You'd better be good to that boy. He's a real catch."

"Why are you assuming everything's my fault?" Molly demanded angrily.

"Because I've met Mark. He's easygoing and sensitive. You are neither of those things." Clara smiled at her daughter. "Now call him and make nice. I'll meet you back in the room."

Molly signed for their breakfast and then dialed Mark's home number. She was put through to voicemail on both his home phone and cell. She dialed the main number at *Collector's Weekly*. Even though she wasn't expecting anyone to answer on a Sunday morning, she knew her mother was right: She couldn't progress with her day until she had tried her best to reach Mark and reconcile with him. After only two rings, Molly was totally shocked when Carl Swanson answered the phone.

"Is that you, Carl?" Molly asked in disbelief.

"I only picked up 'cause I recognized your cell number, Appleby. Damned caller ID is good for something. You looking for your boyfriend, Mr. Marketing Director?"

Molly gulped air. How did Swanson know she and Mark were involved romantically? She thought Clayton was the only person at *Collector's Weekly* who knew that she and Mark were dating. "Um, no," she lied and quickly told Swanson about Cotton nearly being killed. "I may have to stay an extra night. It looks like there are some developments in Tom's case, but nothing definite."

"So stay!" Swanson barked.

"It'll cost us another night in the hotel room, meals, and the price of changing my plane ticket," Molly explained, not wanting to be ranted at by Swanson upon her return for the extra expenses.

"I've got bigger problems than your hotel bill, girlie." Swanson inhaled deeply and Molly could almost see the relief on his face as the nicotine filled his lungs. "You can stay in the presidential suite if you can get a hold of your *boyfriend* and talk him out of this ridiculous career change."

"Career change?" Molly said, bewildered.

Swanson laughed until his laughter turned into a wet, hacking cough. "You don't know, do you?"

Molly clenched her fists with impatient indignation. "Know what?"

"Your *boyfriend* quit. Seems like he's got this crazy notion about going back to medical school." Swanson gave a harsh chuckle. "Guess that's the end of your fancy dinners out. He won't have a penny to throw into a fountain paying med school tuition."

"When did this happen?" she finally said.

"Friday." Her boss sniffed. "Shoot, I can't count on *you* to change Harrison's mind if you didn't even know. Guess he blindsided everyone. His office is already cleared out. And after all I've done for him, he didn't even give me two weeks' notice." Swanson paused. "You'd better rethink gettin' too hot and heavy with someone who pulls a fast one like this." He coughed. "Stay another night, Appleby, but make sure your sweet cheeks are in here first thing Tuesday morning. I'm saving the front page for your piece."

After her boss hung up, Molly listened to the dial tone until a recorded voice indicating that if she would like to make a call, she would need to hang up and try again, forced her back to reality.

Awash in a range of emotions that included hurt, anger, fear, and embarrassment, Molly headed back upstairs to her room. When she opened the door, she was more than ready to fall facedown on the bed and pour out her feelings of betrayal to her mother. But when she saw Clara seated at the desk with the physician's cane on her lap and a pile of tissue paper and bubble wrap strewn about the floor, she found herself unable to speak.

Clara held one of the glass vials between her thumb and index finger so that it caught the light coming from a nearby table lamp. "It's the vial of morphine pills." Clara's eyes flitted back and forth between the vial and her daughter's ashen face. Then she stated the obvious. "They're all gone, honey."

Chapter 11

"Some canes are thinner than a pencil. These are presumed to be ladies' sword canes . . . When the wicked lady would withdraw it from her victim half his insides would come out with it. Isn't that proof that the female is the more bloodthirsty of the species?"

"**N**ow I'll be a suspect!" Molly wailed as she took the cane from her mother's outstretched hand. "What an article me being arrested would make. I'm sure Swanson would promote me to senior staff writer then!"

"You always wanted to be a significant part of a big story. Well, now here's your chance," Clara stated wryly. "By the way, the laudanum wasn't touched—just the morphine."

"Great. Thanks for the sympathy, Ma. Tom was killed by an opium overdose, remember? Morphine pills *are* a form of opium."

Clara reclaimed the cane and stashed it behind the ironing board in the closet. "You have no motive, cupcake, but still, if I were you, I'd keep mum about the empty vial. If that detective gets his meaty hands on it, you might not have it back in time for Easter, let alone Christmas." She paused. "And speaking of gifts for certain boyfriends, how did your tête-à-tête with Mark go?"

"He didn't answer my calls, but you won't *believe* what

he—" Molly stopped as her cell phone began chirping. It was Mark.

"Oh, hello, *Doctor*," Molly gave him an acerbic greeting.

"Uh-oh, Swanson told you," Mark replied mournfully. "Damn that man! I asked him to keep quiet until I could reach you."

"Yeah, what a jerk!" she said, sarcasm dripping from her tongue. "And it was such a *nice* way to find out that my so-called boyfriend quit his job!" Tears sprang into Molly's eyes. "I feel like such an ass! I'm your girlfriend and I'm the *last* person to know!"

"Molly, please," Mark pleaded. "I know you're upset, but this all happened so suddenly and I thought telling Carl first was the right thing, the *professional* thing to do."

"Oh, I'm *so* glad you didn't let your *personal* relationship interfere!" Molly ignored Clara's frantic hand gestures in which her mother raked the air with a pretend pair of claws and hissed, implying that her daughter was acting like a cornered cat. "I thought residencies began in July, anyway. How can you just waltz in now, in October?" Molly demanded icily.

"Um . . ." Mark hesitated and then cleared his throat three times, something he habitually did when he was nervous. "Actually, I've been moonlighting at the hospital for a couple of months now. I, ah, wanted to see if I still wanted to become a physician. And I do." He inhaled as if to gather strength. "It was a decision I wanted to reach without anyone else's influence. I wasn't trying to deceive you."

Molly's shoulders slumped. It all made sense now! Mark's fatigue, his long hours spent reviewing medical textbooks, the dozens of hushed phone conversations from both home and the office—Mark had been planning this move for a long time. "Why didn't you just tell me what was going on?" Molly yelled, anger and hurt surging through her in a wave, rendering her incapable of giving Mark a chance to explain his actions. "I would have encouraged you." She wasn't sure that this was an entirely honest statement so she barreled on. "I guess I don't mean enough to you to deserve to know about a major, life-altering decision."

"Honey, listen. Can we just talk like two adults?"

"No we can't!" she shrieked. "You've had *plenty* of time to talk to me about this! *Months*, apparently. Now *you* can wait until I'm good and ready, which might be next year sometime!"

Clara shook her head violently and mouthed, *"Stop."* Refusing to meet her eyes, Molly marched into the bathroom and slammed the door.

"I'm doing this for us, Molly," Mark jumped in while he had the chance. He didn't realize that his soothing tone only incensed her further. "I want to provide a good life for us."

Normally, such a tender remark would have put Molly at ease, but the stress of the previous forty-eight hours was beginning to bubble up within her. Unable to control herself, she felt pressure rising in her chest like hot steam preparing to burst from a pipe. She longed to scream, but instead, she lowered her voice to a seething whisper. "A good life is built on openness and trust, Mark. I guess those are two things you can't *provide* for me and I need those more than money. Good luck at Duke, *Doctor*." Molly stabbed at the End button on her phone until its text window turned black.

Erupting from the bathroom, she immediately pointed a warning finger at her mother. "Not one word, Ma. I mean it." Molly went over to the mirror, mindlessly fluffed her hair, tugged her ruby-colored turtleneck down over her round hips, and exhaled. "Come on. We've got to get that inventory book. I need to see whether Tom listed the contents of the vials inside my cane and that they were full and unopened. And it's more important than ever that I help solve this case. Not just for Tom, but for me, too. I want that promotion! If Mark's going to quit his job to become a doctor, then I'll show him I can succeed at *my* career without his support."

Clara sadly gathered her purse and opened the hotel room door. "He already knows that you're capable of success, sweetheart. He's always made it clear that he's proud of how smart and talented you are."

"But I'm not significant enough to be his confidante," Molly said and shot her mother a cautionary look. "Let it go, Ma."

"I know you don't want my opinion," Clara pushed on despite a withering glance from Molly, "but before you start looking around for an appropriately sinister suspect, maybe you'd better examine your own behavior. Because the way you handled that phone call was nothing short of criminal!"

The Appleby women only had twenty minutes to investigate Cotton's booth before the show opened and possibly less time than that before Butler and his team arrived in order to search for the inventory book. Unfortunately, Geordie was already manning the booth when the Applebys arrived, his eyes worried and distracted as he dug around in a cardboard box for dustcloths. Extracting two mitts, he waved them in front of Clara.

"What did I do to deserve this kind of suffering?" he moaned and began absently stroking his perfectly-trimmed goatee. "First Tom, now Cotton. My show is going to have a reputation for being haunted! And this booth needs a complete makeover. Oh! I haven't even had time to get my Café Americano this morning. How will I survive?" He clung to Clara's shoulder.

"Let us help," Clara responded, her voice filled with honey. "You go get your espresso or whatever and Molly and I will dust everything and rearrange the smalls before the show opens." When Geordie hesitated, Clara added softly, "Plus, I think you've got a spot on your tie. Better get some club soda on that quick."

"Where?" Geordie looked down, horrified.

Clara, who had rubbed some lipstick onto her index finger moments earlier, picked up Geordie's butter-yellow tie mottled with fat brown polka dots in her hand. She deftly smeared the ruddy pigment over the silk fabric in the pretense of showing him where the stain was located.

"Ohmygod!" Geordie's eyes zeroed in on the spot. "You're right!" He shoved the dusting mitts into Clara's hands. "I'll be back. Don't . . ." He couldn't take his eyes off his tie, which he held away from his chest as though it were contaminated by toxic waste. "Don't *sell* anything big until I get back. I haven't quite figured out why my nephew wants to look over the furniture, but even *I* can't put him off when he's caught the scent of some . . . some crazed murderer!"

Molly watched Geordie hustle off. "That was a low blow, Ma." She laughed, the black cloud above her head dissipating a trace.

"I know it." Clara looked around the booth wildly. "Come on, we don't have much time. Put on one of these mitts. At least we won't leave any fingerprints."

Molly began her search by examining the lines of a deep pine corner cupboard. Old tea tins, candle and butter molds, unusual stoneware crocks, and yellow ware salesman's samples loaded the shelves. She looked over the joinery between the top case and the bottom cabinet, but couldn't find any indication that there was an empty cavity hidden there. She turned her attention to the rough back of the large piece, but the southern yellow pine slats didn't appear to conceal a niche large enough to hide a binder either.

Clara was hastily pulling the small drawers out of a plantation desk whose surface was covered by a display of traveling inkwells. Shaking her head, her mother took out a penlight from her purse and ran the beam along the length of the desk's belly.

"Hurry, Ma!" Molly said as she gave a cursory glance to a cherry chest of drawers before moving on to a stack of steamer trunks. She was momentarily distracted by the weathervanes skillfully mounted on the wall above the chests. There was a brass unicorn, a copper chicken, and a rotund sow made of iron. All of the animals glowed with a warm, metallic patina and bore the evidence of their lengthy exposure to the abuses of Mother Nature. There was also an arrangement of four old trade signs that Molly assumed must be rather expensive—especially the one made of two primitive planks bearing the name of WILLIAMS & SONS FRUITS AND ESSENCE IMPORTERS in faded letters. The central motif of the sign showed a large pineapple in a woven basket along with a cluster of grapes and a bottle of essence of apricot. A pewter tankard and a loaf of bread were painted on the left side of the sign and a few strawberries on a bristly vine embellished the right.

Just as Molly was about to lift the lid on the first trunk, her mother shouted, "I think I've got it!"

Molly dropped the lid with a thunk and scurried over to Clara's side. Her mother's hands were busily rubbing the sides of the cherry chest of drawers Molly had quickly passed over. "Here! See?" Clara placed her daughter's fingers along the base of the chest, where the apron joined the front of the carcass. "It's normal to have a seam here, but I think this apron is actually a false drawer." She reached her fist under the chest and knocked on the bottom. The sound echoed with more hollowness than Molly expected. "Stick your head under the chest and see if there actually is a drawer before I yank the apron right off and cause irreparable damage," Clara ordered.

Molly complied and sank to her knees. She noted how dirty the floor was and wished she hadn't decided to wear her biscuit-colored pants, which had just come back from the dry cleaners. Flattening herself as much as she could, she was appalled to hear Clara whisper, "Hurry, hurry! I see

Geordie heading up the row!" Molly felt a kiss of cold as the skin of her stomach brushed against the cement floor. "Ugh." She shivered and then, forgetting all about her discomfort, she announced, "I see a drawer!"

"Quick! Out of the way!" Clara helped Molly to her knees and then yanked at the bottom of the apron. The entire length of wood pulled away from the case to reveal a skillfully crafted drawer. Inside, the inventory book glowed neon orange. Clara grabbed the book, shoved it inside Molly's cavernous bag, and stood up just as Geordie returned, brandishing a silver thermos and a new tie the color of huckleberries.

"Oh!" Clara gushed. "What a fabulous tie! We're all set with the dusting, but we didn't have a chance to rearrange anything yet. Do you want us to stay and help?"

Geordie's eyes were locked on the dirty patches on the knees of Molly's pants. "No, no." He shooed them off. "Thank you, but no. There's nothing I enjoy better than futzing around someone else's booth. Besides, Cotton's wife is coming over in a jiffy. She said there's nothing she can do to help Cotton while he's under sedation so she might as well make a little money." Geordie giggled. "Is that woman a prize or what?"

Molly and Clara agreed and then dashed away, hoping to examine the book before Butler and his crew discovered that it was missing.

"They'll *never* think to look behind that apron!" Clara declared triumphantly.

Molly was just about to congratulate her mother for discovering the hidden drawer when she saw something that rendered her speechless. Passing by the Geese in the Wind booth containing antique quilts and other textiles, she was thunderstruck to see Becky Ross with her arms wrapped around the expensively clad figure of Howard Rose. As the couple had their eyes closed and were kissing passionately, they didn't see Molly's jaw drop open as she hustled her prattling mother past the booth. Once they reached the safety of the hallway, she considered mentioning the little display of public affection she had just witnessed, but an idea occurred to her that immediately displaced the image of the lip-locked dealers.

"What we need right now," Molly looked around nervously, "is a copier. Then we can look over the pages without having to worry about Butler discovering we took the book. Let's go to one of the lobbies and see if we can borrow one of the hotel's machines."

The two women power-walked down the carpeted halls. Clara seemed to be enjoying herself immensely, but the pain Molly felt over Mark was still raw. Now she was covered with dust and, once again, unhappily aware how out of shape she was. In fact, just as she decided to ask her mother to ease her frantic pace she spied the form of Detective Butler followed by two uniformed policemen coming down the hall straight for them. Looking around, Molly saw that there was only one set of doors she and Clara could enter if they wanted to avoid being seen by Butler.

"Ma! In here!" She grabbed her mother's elbow and pulled her through the first door on their right.

"What are you—?" Clara stopped as the two women practically fell into the arms of the three men they had seen on the third floor earlier that morning. Molly recognized their baseball caps and friendly, open faces immediately.

"Well, shucks!" the one wearing the Stihl hat bellowed. "You little ladies here for the turkey hunter's convention? Just knock me down and steal my teeth. I'd never have taken y'all for members of the National Wild Turkey Federation." He eyed Molly's hands. "You wearing special huntin' gloves or somethin'?"

"Um, actually we're not *exactly* members." Molly smiled. "But it sounds like a lot of fun." She removed the mitts from her hands. "These are for dusting. I forgot to take them off."

"Y'all are here just in time, too," the man whose name was Buddy seemed not to hear Molly as he clapped her on the back so heartily she thought her breakfast was in danger of coming back up her throat. "The owl-hootin' competition is gettin' started." Buddy gestured toward the front of the room where a man stepped up to the microphone and began reviewing the rules of the competition. "We've only got three seats saved, but I'm sure the fellows would make room for such fine outdoor women as yourselves."

"Too bad you can't do an owl hoot, Buddy," one of his companions said. "They're givin' out a mighty nice ring to the winners." He turned to Molly and raised his furry eyebrows suggestively. "Might impress the ladies, winnin' that ring."

Buddy took a step closer to Molly and smiled. "I did purty good in the gobble contest yesterday. I was one of five winners and made me a nice pile of money. How about I take you two out for supper later?"

"Sorry," Clara jumped in. "We're catching a plane in an hour. Thanks, though. Gotta run!" And the two women made their exit as the first contestant began to exhibit his owl-hooting talents.

At the concierge desk, Clara swiftly sweet-talked her way into having the contents of the inventory book copied. Within minutes, the tired women were once again inside the Heart of Dixie show. They furtively made their way back to Cotton's booth hoping to avoid detection. As they rounded the corner leading to Cotton's row, Molly ran smack into a man's muscular chest and promptly ricocheted into her mother.

"In a hurry?" Detective Butler, owner of the steel torso, asked.

"Um . . ." Molly began, shoving the dusting mitts in her back pocket.

Butler gave her a perplexed look. "Mrs. Leitts told me

where the book is stashed and I'm on my way to get it, so if you'll excuse me."

Molly took her bag off her shoulder and pushed it into Clara's arms. "That's great news, but I need to tell you something before you go. Please, it's very important." She put her hand on the small of her mother's back and shoved. "I'll meet you later in Grayson's booth to look at that *book* you were interested in buying."

Clara understood that Molly meant to stall Butler so that she, Clara, could return Tom's binder to its secret drawer. Waving goodbye, she hurried off.

"Sorry, but I don't want my mom to worry." Molly smiled sheepishly while Butler bored holes through her skull with his eyes. "I wanted you to know that I bought a cane from Tom's booth on Saturday. It was a physician's cane and had two vials of drugs inside of it." She took a deep breath and plowed ahead. "One was laudanum and the second, morphine pills. The vials were unopened."

"Yes?" Butler shifted impatiently.

"The morphine pills are gone. Stolen."

Butler stared at her hard and then reached for his cell phone. "You still have that tray of coffee you told me about earlier?" he asked her.

Molly nodded. "Yes, unless room service cleaned it up, but I doubt they would have as I asked that the tray not be removed."

"Bro?" Butler spoke into his cell phone. "I'm going to need another rush analysis. A pot of coffee." He paused. "Well, it's possible that the killer put poison in the Applebys' coffee. Yeah, she found the body." He paused. "Yep, opium again, but don't leap to any conclusions until you've done your thing." He listened, glancing at Molly. "Sure, I'll have her meet you up in room . . . ?" He hesitated until Molly provided her room number. He then passed the number on to his brother and snapped his phone shut.

"Can you wait there until my brother arrives?" he inquired less abruptly. "I'll be up as soon as I'm done down here."

Molly nodded again, feeling a numbness creep up her legs. Was she the killer's next target?

Butler steadied her by clamping his hands on her shoulders. "I'll join you after I've collected the book. If someone *is* after you, then it's because you know something. And if you know something vital to this case, then *I* need to know it, too." His fingers squeezed slightly harder. "Go straight to your room. No detours. Understood?"

"Yes," Molly whimpered beneath the force of his intent gaze and iron grip. Then she remembered the sheaf of papers folded inside her bag. She wanted a chance to look them over before Butler did. If someone *had* tried to poison her coffee, she damned well wanted to know who. "I'll go up to my room," she said, her voice gathering strength, as she stood up as tall and erect as possible, gaining a slight height advantage over the detective. "Really," she said with false sweetness. "Promise."

The woman sat in a leather wing chair with her feet propped up on a needlepoint footstool, leisurely reading in front of a gas log fire. The book, Decorating with French Country Antiques *was so filled with scrap-paper bookmarks sticking out in every direction that it began to resemble a paper porcupine. A notebook filled with hurried, messy handwriting lay open on a nineteenth-century walnut candle stand and a saucer bearing a delicately flowered teacup rested without a coaster next to the notebook. The woman took a sip of lukewarm tea, scowled, and replaced the teacup roughly, so that tea slapped over the edge of the saucer onto the perfect patina of the candle stand's surface.*

"Oh damn," the woman muttered, carelessly wiping at the stain with her sleeve. Her expensive blouse, made of hand-woven silk, was already dappled with minute splotches of ink, for the woman was unaware that her ballpoint pen had a small leak. Each time she raised it to her mouth to gnaw at the tip, a habit she had developed as a child and

had never outgrown, small flecks of black mottled both sides of the lavender-colored silk neckline adjoining a costly necklace made of a triple strand of Mikimoto pearls secured by a diamond clasp in the shape of a fleur-de-lis.

Kicking off a pair of silver Prada sandals, the woman ran a hand through her immensely thick honey-brown hair and for the first time, noticed the ink stains on her blouse. Shrugging in a bemused fashion at her own heedlessness, she got up and headed into the bedroom to change. She tugged off the blouse in distaste, threw it on a large mound of soiled clothing on the floor of her closet, and pulled on a pink cashmere sweater. She began to walk while the sweater was only partway on, obscuring her view so that she banged her knee roughly against one of her husband's many cane racks fashioned of heavy Victorian oak.

"God, I hate these canes!" she seethed, aiming a direct but ineffectual kick at the cane rack. "What a ridiculously stupid collection. You're all going!" she announced to the dozen canes protruding from the closest rack like an army of umbrellas awaiting rain. "All of you!" The woman chuckled to herself. "Yes indeed, Mrs. Frazier has come into some money and Mrs. Frazier is going to redecorate. And if Mr. Frazier doesn't like it, well that's just too bad."

The woman lingered in the hall, running slender fingers over the ivory knob of a seventeenth-century walking stick. "Ugly," she whispered to it, and then picked up a folk art cane with a curved handle depicting Jonah being swallowed by the whale. She ignored the fine carving, the shock and surprise registered on Jonah's face; the hungry greed carved into the whale's painted eyes. She replaced it in its slot with a bang. "Ugly," she taunted. Finally, she moved on to the kitchen, where she put the kettle on to boil.

She passed right by her husband's mounted display case where he stored his five favorite and most valuable gadget canes. His treasures rested beneath glass on a soft bed of crimson velvet. If she had paid those particular canes any *notice, she would have seen that there was an empty space within one of the display cases; a depression in the velvet upon which a cane once rested. Instead, the woman stood over the stove waiting for the water to boil, a clean porcelain teacup waiting to be filled. She munched on a chocolate biscotti, her teeth biting forcefully into the cookie as crumbs tumbled lightly down her sweater and onto the floor.*

She heard a floorboard creak somewhere in the house but paid no mind to the familiar sound. The house she shared with her husband was fifty years old and the floors were made of heart of pine salvaged from a nineteenth-century farmhouse, so they groaned and settled upon themselves from time to time. The woman bit into another biscotti. Another board creaked, closer this time. She swung around and jumped, suddenly startled.

"What are you . . . ?" she began with a dismissive tone to her voice, and then her eyes grew round with surprise and a trace of fear. Before she could utter another word, a blade as thin as a paper's edge darted out of the wooden cobra's hood that formed the handle of her husband's missing cane. The dagger punctured her jugular with a whispered hiss, and then withdrew once again into its secret recess.

The woman put a hand to her throat where blood was already flowing freely down her neck, onto her sweater, and onto the pine floor. It trickled down into the cracks between the boards and began to pool in one of the dark knots of pine beneath her silver sandals. She tried to speak, but only a series of shocked gurgles issued forth from her open mouth.

Suddenly, the doorbell rang. The killer listened and then calmly pressed a hidden release on the back of the cobra's head and a second, invisible lever on the front of the reptile's neck. The deadly blade was once more exposed. Keeping a finger firmly pressed on the two buttons, the killer then carefully wiped the blade clean using a kitchen towel decorated with a parade of roosters, stepped over the woman's prostrate body, replaced the cane in its display case, and left the house through the back door.

The kettle began to scream.

Chapter 12

"While animal, reptile, and insect denizens of the forest all appear on folk art walking sticks, the sinuous snake is most often featured. The long, lazy S shapes of many branches just beg to be transformed into snakes."

JEFFREY B. SNYDER, CANES AND WALKING STICKS

Molly was shocked to see that her mother had removed the copies of Tom's inventory list from her purse and was leafing through them as Grayson and Belinda each chatted with a customer. Clara barely glanced up when Molly whispered angrily, "What are you doing? You couldn't wait a few minutes for me?" She looked around to make sure no one could hear her. "Did you put the original back?"

Clara nodded. "Luckily, Geordie was tied up with a local reporter. And speaking of hiding things . . ." She gestured at the game table, where Molly and Belinda had played backgammon the day before. The charming game set must have been sold earlier as a wooden chessboard and its hand-carved pieces featuring nautical themes had taken over the prime location on the table surface. "Not the chess set. Look under the table."

Molly carefully raised one of the dropped leaves of the game table and saw a blanketed shape squatting in the darkness below. "Is that the dower chest?"

"Yes. But now we can deliver it back to Darlene as it *was* Tom's to sell all along." She shook the sheaf of papers. "Tom has copies of the McPhees' divorce settlement. *All* household items belonged to Mrs. McPhee, regardless of who originally paid for them. She sold the chest and a dozen smalls to Tom for peanuts. I guess she just wanted the things out of her sight." Clara's eyes twinkled. "Wait until we tell Charity! If she sells that chest through Lex, she'll make enough to save her house! Lex can put a nice chunk of change in his own bank account and *I* might even be given a nice little finder's fee. I hope so, because that would pay for that gorgeous Auman pottery vase I bought last month. Isn't that great news?"

Molly frowned. "You know," she whispered, "there's a grim possibility that Charity knew about these documents all along. With Tom dead, she may get every cent of the profits from the sale of the chest and from the rest of Tom's inventory as well. I bet she knows exactly how Tom's will reads."

"She didn't do it," Clara said, standing.

"How do we know?" Molly insisted. "This would be the perfect setting to bump off her ex. With all the dealers and customers coming and going, anyone could have stolen opium from Tom's booth. It makes things awfully tough on the police. There would be no clear prints. Plus, she claims she was out walking when Cotton was stabbed and supposedly asleep when Tom was killed. Pretty weak alibis."

Clara waved goodbye to Grayson and Belinda and headed toward the All That Glitters booth. "It's not her," Clara said.

"Why not? She's obviously interested in money so she had the motive. She knew that Tom's inventory included antique pieces that still contained their original poisons, *and* she knew that Tom was having heart problems. All she had to do was spike his margarita. We know that she and

Tom argued early Friday night, so she was close enough to him to slip some opium in his drink."

"Molly!" Clara was exasperated.

"Look, I know that you identify with Charity because you both share that irresponsible husband connection, but even if Charity killed Tom to protect the welfare of her children, it's wrong."

Clara's lip drew into a thin line. "This is not about *me*, Molly. This is about logic. Grayson overheard Tom talking to Cotton about a man. Cotton had said, 'I'm afraid *he* saw me,' so he wasn't talking about Charity. I'm more certain than ever that Howard Rose is our bad guy."

"I don't know," Molly countered. "I think Rose may have been busy with . . . ah . . . *other* activities Friday night. I don't know about Saturday, but whoever killed Tom must have been the same person to stab Cotton." She slowed as they approached All That Glitters. "Tell Charity quickly, Ma. We've got to meet Butler's brother in our room so that he can check out that second pot of coffee."

"And take your cane away, no doubt." Clara waved at Charity as they entered the booth. Charity was showing a customer an antique heart-shaped pendant encrusted with diamonds and rose-colored pearls. She excused herself, waited for Nell to help the entranced customer, and then linked arms with Clara. "You look like you're going to make my day. I could use a bit of cheering up, so please tell me you've got some positive news."

"Do I ever!" Clara told Charity all about the divorce papers. "But don't let on to that detective that I told you. We're not supposed to have been snooping through that book."

"My lips are sealed," Charity promised. "Or at least until that scumbag Rose makes an appearance. I'm going to have one of the porters bring the chest back to Tom's booth. That ought to bring Rose running like my kids when they hear the ice cream truck." She hugged both Molly and Clara. "Thank you so much. And Clara, you tell Lex that the sale of Tom's inventory is his as soon as all the legalities are cleared up. I talked to my lawyer last night, who happens to be Tom's lawyer, too—we live in a small town—and he told me that Tom left everything to Tom Jr. and Ashley, with me as the executor. But it looks like the estate will be frozen as long as the police are still investigating his death. When his assets have finally thawed, so to speak, I'll sign a contract with Lex. I know you'll do your best by me and my kids . . . and Tom's memory. You've already proved to be a true friend."

Clara's eyes glistened. "Lex and I will take care of you, don't worry. Right now, though, we'd better run. We've got another date with the cops."

"Well, I hope you can help them figure out what happened to Tom!" Charity called out. "I need to make up two mortgage payments and fast!"

"God, that woman has a one-track mind," Molly huffed. "But I agree, she's probably not the killer. It's in her best interest financially for Tom to have died naturally. Who knows when she'll get control of his estate now? The police may never solve this crime."

Clara looked surprised. "That isn't like you, madam. You are always determined to see a mystery to its end. I know you're upset about Mark, but I thought you wanted to write a one-of-a-kind piece on this show." She absently stroked her chin as they walked, her forehead furrowed in thought. "So what about Rose?"

"He may have a decent alibi for Friday night. I think he and Becky Ross are an item," Molly said and then explained how she had seen the couple kissing and described the hickeys she had seen on Becky's neck Saturday night at the Irish bar.

"Oh dear." Clara clucked in amusement. "I doubt *Mrs.* Rose would be happy to learn about her husband's extracurricular activities at this show. However, we don't know how long he was with Becky that night." She smirked. "He could be one of those five-minute men."

"Ma!" Molly had to laugh. "Where do you get this stuff?" As they walked passed the Country Doctor, Darlene hailed them over, her eyes wide with fear.

"You've got to help me!" she squawked. "That awful Howard Rose yelled at me so horribly when he saw that the chest wasn't here in the booth. What am I supposed to tell him?" She looked down the aisle as if expecting to see an executioner, complete with black hood and sharp axe, marching toward her. "He's going to bring Mr. Alexis *and* security back with him!"

"He can bring a brass band for all the good it'll do him," Clara snorted. "Keep an eye on things, Molly. I'm going to take a walk with Darlene and get her up to speed. There are hardly any customers left in here, anyway. It's almost wrap time."

As Clara meandered off with Darlene, Molly took the opportunity of being alone to leaf through Tom's inventory pages. Just as she suspected, the details of her physician's cane were listed in black-and-white.

"Maybe some other antique is missing its opium vial," she muttered to herself and began to glance through the pages until she found the listing for the apothecary boxes. There were three boxes altogether and despite the fact that Molly knew she should be heading upstairs to meet Berkley Butler in her room, she began to compare the contents of each box with those listed on the inventory sheets. The first two boxes matched perfectly and clearly nothing had been taken from either one, but the third was missing an item: a small glass bottle of Dover's Powder.

"Dover's Powder?" Molly wondered aloud.

"It's a mixture of opium, syrup of ipecac, and potassium sulfate." Detective Butler responded from behind her.

Molly jumped, dropping the inventory sheets. They

fluttered toward the floor and scattered on the slick cement as if swept by a broom. Butler followed their movement with his eyes. She wilted beneath his smoldering gaze.

"Investigating murder is not a game, Miss Appleby." He pointed at the strewn pages. "Why are you trying so hard to stay one step ahead of me? Don't you realize that you're playing with fire? One man's dead, another's barely escaped with his life, and for all we know, the killer's now set his sights on *you*."

Molly anxiously tore at her fingernails. "I'm sorry. I *was* going to tell you if I found out anything crucial."

"When? *After* your article was published? Oh, you're a clever one, finding the binder and then copying the pages, I'll give you that, but I've got a few more resources and a hell of a lot more experience going after criminals than you do." Butler examined the contents of the third apothecary box. He peered morosely at the empty space among the row of small glass bottles with their cork stoppers. "According to my brother, Dover's Powder was used to induce sweating. It was invented by an English doc in the eighteenth century who believed that a person could sweat away an illness. It was like an antique cold remedy. I guess folks in our country still used the stuff throughout most of the next century." He closed the lid to the box. "Unfortunately for Tom, opium in a powdered form has a *long* shelf life. And an entire bottle mixed into a drink could kill a man with a strong and healthy heart, which we both know Tom didn't have."

"Why are you telling me this?" Molly asked with trepidation.

"Did you kill Tom Barnett?" Butler demanded harshly.

Molly felt as though she had been slapped. "Of course not! I—"

Butler cut her off. "Did your mother kill Tom Barnett?"

"No!"

"Well, one of you antique people did." He looked at his

watch. "And I've only got a few hours left before this show ends and people start packing up and heading home." He jabbed his finger at a page inside the orange binder. "Right now, there are *two* items missing from this booth: the bottle of Dover's Powder and some kind of walking stick." He stared hard at Molly. "You seem have an interest in these sticks. You bought one yesterday. Do you remember seeing a stick that fits this description, either in this booth or being carried around by someone?"

Molly examined the typed paragraph describing the missing walking stick.

> Folk art walking stick featuring a carved cobra head with bared fangs. Eyes made of white stones. Exceptional carving detail all over handle, especially in regards to the many scales. Metal collar. Shaft is made of ash with evidence of burn marks most likely caused by lightning. Early 19th century. Mint condition. Continental. As with most folk art sticks, there is no ferrule. **$695 firm**
>
> *(Purchased 6/10/04 from Mebane Auction, NC,*
> *for $440)*

"There's a check mark next to the description, see?" Butler pointed out. "Barnett made the same mark next to all of the items he brought to this show. According to Darlene, the rest of this stuff is back at his shop in Virginia. Now, she's got receipts for everything that's been sold this weekend, but there's no record of anyone buying this stick or cane."

"I don't remember seeing it on Friday night, and I looked over all of the canes displayed in here." Molly walked over to the umbrella stand. "But the booth was a mess that night. That snake stick could have been in a piece of furniture, in Tom's van, or his room. Maybe he forgot to unpack it. I think I would have noticed it on Saturday if it were here. It sounds like an unusual piece. I've never seen a snake cane where there was an open mouth with fangs and such."

At that moment, Butler's cell phone beeped. He read the incoming text message. "My brother got the coffeepot from your room and is headed back to the lab," He typed in a speedy reply and then shoved his phone back into his pocket. "And no, the stick isn't in Tom's room or his van. It's not in your room, either."

Molly blinked in surprise. "What?"

"Don't worry, I'm not picking on you. My men are searching the hotel rooms and vehicles of everyone connected to this show for the two items missing from this booth. No one gets to pack up tonight without being supervised by a member of the Nashville PD." The detective made this pronouncement with authority, but the worry in his eyes was evident.

"Why are you even interested in the snake cane?" Molly wondered.

"Because it's a loose end, and in my experience, loose ends mean something." He paused to pick up a cane with a carved ivory skull handle. "In murder investigations, one little detail can make or break the case."

"What about Cotton? Is he still asleep?" She shared in the detective's frustration. "He *must* know something helpful."

Butler dropped the skull cane back into the umbrella rack. "He's a bit groggy, but was coherent enough to write down answers to my questions. That poor guy isn't going to be talking for a while. Such an unusual wound." He sighed, exasperated. "He couldn't help me, though. All he saw was a dark shape in his room and then felt the pain in his throat."

Molly frowned. "But why was Cotton attacked in the first place? Was it because of what Tom told him Friday night at the Jack Daniel's Saloon? That Tom had been at the wrong place at the wrong time and had seen something dangerous?"

Butler threw his hands up in the air. "There's *more* information you've withheld from me! I ought to throw you in jail for obstruction, just to teach you a lesson! Lord," he looked up to the ceiling in appeal, "spare me from amateurs!"

Backing away from Butler's growl, Molly said, "I didn't say anything because all that conversation told me was that the killer was a man!" She panted, "Didn't Tom tell Cotton the name of this guy he witnessed doing something . . . bad?"

Butler kicked at the floor and muttered, "No. Tom told Cotton that it would be safer if he didn't mention any names. He just gave Cotton the inventory book to hold until he could figure out what to do."

Molly grew silent. It was looking grim for the detective, and for her as well. The minutes were ticking away until the show would be over. "I think the most likely suspect is Howard Rose. He really wanted that dower chest."

"Rose was with the governor until very late Saturday night and spent Friday night with a lady friend. He and his lady were spotted in a restaurant downtown and then checked into a bed-and-breakfast for the evening. The owner saw them go up to their room at eleven and neither one reappeared until after seven the next morning. Rose is clear."

"I'm sorry." Molly looked down at her hands, feeling ashamed. "I *was* trying to figure this out for myself, but I promise that I don't know anything else. I thought finding the inventory book would solve all of the riddles." Her eye traveled around the booth. "I guess there's no hope of finding a nice set of prints on this apothecary box or on the margarita glass Tom was poisoned with, is there?"

Butler shook his head. "The only prints on the glass are yours. The glass had been wiped clean. God knows how many people have touched this box since the show started, but I'd bet my badge that the killer left no traces here either. No, prints won't help. We need the bottle or the stick."

"Is there anything I can do to help?" Molly inquired meekly.

"Yeah!" Butler shouted. "Go to your room and stay there!"

A few hours later, Molly closed the lid to her laptop. She had e-mailed Carl the Heart of Dixie article, including the frightning conclusion that the killer who had attacked two dealers had yet to be apprehended. She would write the other Nashville piece featuring the tailgate show upon her return to Durham.

Clara snapped shut the paperback she had been reading and sighed. "I like this Lord Ambrose fellow. He's scarred, hermitlike, rich, and completely eccentric. It's like having Mr. Rochester and Sherlock Holmes wrapped into one person. Have you got the second book in the series?"

Molly shook her head. "Not yet; it's on order. Speaking of orders, I wonder what happened with the coffeepot Detective Butler's brother picked up."

Clara suddenly grew very interested in the blurb written on the back of her book.

"Ma?"

"I didn't want to ruin your day any further, honey. I talked to the *other* Butler after my little stroll with Darlene. He found opium in that coffeepot. Enough to put us out of commission for a few days." She fanned the books pages in her hand and mumbled, "Or maybe longer."

Molly jumped up. "So the killer *is* after us!" She checked the lock on the door and applied the chain with shaking fingers. "What are we going to do?"

"Look outside the door," Clara replied calmly. "I think you'll find we're under police protection."

"Whew," Molly said, waving to the bored officer seated on an uncomfortable metal folding chair in the hallway. "Still, no room service for us tonight. Let's eat at that Italian restaurant in the Garden section. It's got such a soothing atmosphere with soft lights, calm music, and a signature tiramisu. I could go for some veal tortellini tossed in a creamy cheese sauce and a big heel of homemade bread."

"And a huge cocktail," Clara added. "I mean, my glass had better be the size of a fishbowl."

"What are we going to do once we get home, Ma?" Molly fretted after giving the waiter her order. Despite the calm and romantic setting Ristorante Volare provided, Molly was unable to relax. She kept examining the faces of the other diners, searching for traces of latent violence in the body language or in the eyes of the strangers seated around her. None of the other dealers were present. Those who lived within driving distance had already packed up, and having obtained permission from the police, promptly left Nashville. Only a small handful were staying over another night with plans to leave early the next morning. Molly couldn't help but wonder: Was the killer gone or was he still in the hotel somewhere, watching?

"Neither of us have alarms in our houses," she reminded Clara. "We don't even have big dogs. Unless I cover the killer with Reddi-wip, my cats won't bother themselves by attacking him."

"I've always got the option of staying with Lex and Kitty, but they only have one spare bed, so there's only one choice left for you," Clara said, ripping off a chunk of warm bread from a napkin-lined basket. "You'll have to make up with Mark and move in with him until things are safe again."

Molly stopped chewing. "Fat chance. I'm not quite

ready to let Mark off the hook. Besides, Butler will have his man before we board the plane tomorrow. He's got the best track record in the state for closing cases, remember?"

Clara ordered a second cocktail. "Right," she said dubiously. When the waiter returned with her drink, she took a mighty swallow.

Chapter 13

Straight canes with multiple inner lives do not want to attract attention. This explains why many of them were not kept after the owner passed away, they were either removed or banished to the attic. There they were found by children, their secrets were detected and their content was dispersed, broken or lost.

ULRICH KLEVER, WALKINGSTICKS

Early Monday morning Molly was brushing her teeth with her new electronic toothbrush when the sound of forceful knocking on her hotel room door made her jump. The sudden movement caused the toothbrush to pop out of her mouth and vibrate madly in the air, thoroughly spraying Molly's black turtleneck sweater with Aquafresh.

Swallowing a laugh as she passed the bathroom, Clara opened the door to Detective Butler.

"Good morning, ladies." Butler tried to sound upbeat but the weariness in his face and the look of defeat in his eyes betrayed his true feelings. "I wanted a word with you before you left for the airport."

Clara took a seat in one of the room's two chairs while Molly stood nearby, dabbing helplessly at her sweater with a damp washcloth.

Butler also remained standing, but his body sagged against the desk and he took a long sip of coffee from a large, insulated travel cup before speaking again. "As of today, we have yet to make any arrests. Without going into further detail on how the case stands at the moment, I've come to give you a warning." He glanced at both women. "Since you listed different towns as addresses on your statements, I assume that you don't exactly live next door to one another. Do you both live alone?"

Molly nodded while Clara said, "If you can count seven cats taking up every chair, couch, countertop, and available bed alone, then yes."

"What about alarm systems?" Butler continued, ignoring Clara's flippant response.

"Neither of us," Molly answered.

"But!" Clara piped up. "I *do* have my father's old shotgun and I'd love an excuse to use it. I'm sure I'm still a great shot." She paused. "I guess I should clean it, though. It hasn't been oiled in over ten years."

Butler balled his fists in annoyance. "I don't know why I'm bothering with you two. I should hand out your addresses on fliers and *hope* that this nutcase finds you."

Clara's eyes grew huge. Butler looked instantly remorseful and subsequently began rubbing his head in a most agitated manner. Molly expected sparks to ignite on the tips of the detective's short hair. "Sorry," he said, "but seriously, you should both find other places to live until we nail this guy. I've got leads—so don't get too worried. And I still can't figure out why the killer tried to take you out in the first place, but be on your guard." He glared at Molly. "No early morning walks in the deep woods or late-night strolls in empty parking lots, got it?"

"Yes, sir." Molly took his outstretched hand and shook it. "I've learned my lesson about detecting. I'm obviously no good at it."

Butler shifted uneasily on his feet. "All right, then. One of my guys is going to run you to the airport. He's waiting outside in a squad car. Now, you've got my card, so call me if anything comes up. I've got a few more dealers to talk to before they hightail it outta here, so take care."

"We will, thank you, Detective. Good luck!" Molly closed the door and finished packing her suitcase. The phone rang and Clara answered it. She murmured into the receiver, glanced at her watch, and then said, "All right. See you in a bit."

Molly heaved her bag off the bed and gave one last swipe at her sweater with the washcloth. "Who was that?"

"Grayson," Clara replied and suddenly became very busy packing her cosmetic bag. "He's ordered a light breakfast for us and has it set out in his room. I told him we've only got a few minutes, but I'd rather eat the hotel's food than some fast-food junk at the airport."

"That's fine. I'm sure we won't be late for our flight anyway." Molly smiled. "If there's any traffic, our police escort can turn on the sirens and ride on the shoulder."

Clara propped open the hotel room door and waved Molly onward. "Let's go, madam. I've had it with Nashville. I can't wait to go home and kiss my cats."

Grayson opened the door to his suite wearing a maroon smoking jacket over a white dress shirt and charcoal slacks. Molly didn't even know that smoking jackets were still available for sale, but she thought Grayson looked more like Sean Connery than ever in such an aristocratic piece of clothing.

"Good morning, ladies." He gestured toward the balcony. "I thought we'd breakfast outside. Might as well enjoy the scenery for a few moments longer."

Examining the cluttered surface of the linen-covered table on Grayson's balcony, it appeared as though he had ordered a sampling of the entire menu. There was a rasher of bacon, a deep dish of scrambled eggs, slabs of ham, a tall stack of pancakes and another of Belgian waffles, an assortment of toast and rolls, and a basket of cinnamon buns.

"What? No grits?" Clara teased, but Grayson instantly sprang to a set of covered bowls set up on a side table and whipped off the covers. One bowl contained grits and the other, oatmeal. Clara gestured at the feast. "Have you invited all the members of the Turkey Hunters convention, too?"

"I didn't know what your favorite breakfast food was, so I just ordered a bit of everything," Grayson admitted sheepishly, pulling out a chair for Clara.

Clara poured coffee into the three cups set out on the table. "Actually, I like grits and Swedish pancakes from IHOP the most, so you've got one out of two."

"Ah, Swedish pancakes with lingonberries," Grayson mused. "I enjoy those as well."

Another score for Grayson, Molly thought, piling generous portions of bacon, eggs, and raisin toast onto her plate. She would start her diet on Tuesday for certain.

"There's a specific reason I asked you both to join me before you left for the airport," Grayson said after the two women had eaten their fill. "I would like to offer you my home in Charleston as a refuge until the individual responsible for this weekend's unfortunate events is apprehended. I am leaving for a buying trip in England and the house will be empty, but it has an advanced security system and a guard routinely drives by the property." He took Clara's hand. "There is a flight to Charleston leaving just minutes after your scheduled flight to Raleigh-Durham. I can have you both on that flight with one quick call. You can buy clothes and whatever else you require for a longer stay once you reach my home. I'll have a driver at your disposal." He gazed at Clara fondly. "I cannot express how much it means to me that both of you remain safe."

Clara returned Grayson's affectionate look but removed

her hand from his. "That is such a nice offer, Grayson, and at any other time I would gladly accept. I love Charleston! But I have to work. We've got a big catalog sale coming up and there's a rumor that the Hogg family is going to sell their ancestral home with all of its contents. Lex has been in contact with the family, but they'd like me to be present when the contract terms are discussed." She rubbed her hands together in anticipation. "It's the kind of sale I've dreamed about and I've *got* to be in Hillsborough to close the deal." She scowled fiercely. "Besides, no one is going to force me to change my behavior. Not even a murderer," she added with conviction. "He'd better watch out if he interferes with the Hogg contract. I've got a big gun and I know how to use it."

Grayson chuckled. "Somehow, that was the answer I expected, so I've contacted a friend of mine. He's a former FBI field agent. Retired now, but he takes on an occasional job." He paused, studying both women. "I've hired him to keep an eye on your houses. He'll be in a dark blue Cadillac, so if you see one patrolling your street, that's my friend Roy."

"That is very kind of you, Mr. Montgomery. Thank you." Molly spoke up as her mother seemed to be at a loss for words.

"This is for *my* peace of mind, more than anything," he said graciously. "I'll enjoy my trip abroad much more knowing that someone is looking after you both."

Clara stood, obviously flustered. "We really should go. Thank you, Grayson."

Grayson also rose and then leaned over and kissed Clara softly on the cheek. "Look after yourself until I return."

Clara flushed and headed for the door.

"One moment, Molly." Grayson touched her on the arm and spoke very softly. "I can see that you and your mother have a close relationship. Therefore, I would like to ask your permission to, well, to use an old-fashioned term, to court Clara. She is the most remarkable woman I have ever met."

Molly beamed. "Of course! Give it your best shot, Mr. Montgomery. I'm behind you all the way."

"Please, call me Grayson. And I have a gift for you." He placed a book-shaped package wrapped in red tissue paper in her hands. "No need to open it now. It's just a small token. Your mother mentioned that you enjoyed the writing of Agatha Christie and I figured after the weekend you've had, you deserve a little treat. Have a safe flight home."

Inside the squad car, Clara released a heavy sigh. "That man is something else! What did he say to you while we were leaving?"

"He wants to date you, Ma, and he asked for my blessing. I gave it to him, naturally. You'd be an idiot not to at least give him a chance."

Clara shrugged. "Who said I wasn't going to? He likes cats, after all."

"He has quite a list of admirable qualities," Molly said. "He also gave me this." She held out the wrapped parcel.

"As a bribe?" Clara issued a mock frown.

"I highly doubt it. I had already told him to abduct you if necessary." She tore off the tissue and examined the book. "Wow," she breathed. It was a signed first edition copy of *The ABC Murders*. "Ma, your boyfriend is so cool."

"Boyfriend!" Clara took the book from Molly's hands. "Ugh. *That's* going to take some getting used to."

As it turned out, there was absolutely no need for the twentysomething officer driving the Applebys to the airport to employ his siren, though it looked as though nothing would have pleased him more. In between telling the two women why he had joined the force, Officer Reynolds casually imparted the news that most of the flights departing from Nashville International were delayed due to a front of heavy rains bearing down from the plains states.

"A perfect ending to a miserable trip," Molly stated glumly. She hated sitting around at airports and didn't want too much dead time on her hands. If she wasn't busy, she'd start thinking about Mark. Her anger toward Mark would then cause her to rehash her failure to help Detective Butler find the Heart of Dixie Killer. The two subjects were likely to cause her to spiral into a state of complete depression.

Officer Reynolds insisted on accompanying the women to their gate, despite their protests that there was plenty of security in the airport already. As the threesome approached the boarding area, Molly was relieved to see that their flight had not yet been delayed. If they were lucky, they'd be airborne within the next half-hour.

Molly thanked the young officer and joined her mother in one of the few available seats. Disgruntled passengers were complaining loudly on cell and pay phones about their tardy flights while bored and restless children ran wildly about the area, their parents too tired to correct the rowdy behavior. Most of the people seated around them had their faces hidden in books and newspapers and only surfaced to take giant gulps of coffee, glance with irritation at their watches, or to shoot dirty looks at the gate attendants as if the men and women were personally responsible for the inclement weather.

Clearly excited by the possibility that one of these unhappy travelers might suddenly become hostile, Reynolds began strolling around the boarding area, darting sharp glances at the wayward children or invading the personal space of those being too vociferous on their cell phones.

"Now that's a good cop," Molly declared. She quickly changed her mind, however, as Reynolds began to aggressively question the passenger who had just arrived to their gate via electric car. The skycap handling the passenger's luggage momentarily blocked Molly's view, but as he stepped aside, she was able to see Dennis Frazier. The expression on his face was a combination of puzzlement and dismay as Reynolds pointed repeatedly at Frazier's cane and then began to furiously punch numbers into his cell phone. Molly hustled over to Dennis's side, prepared to defend him against the zealous officer.

"Are you okay?" she asked him. "What's going on?"

"This young policeman seems to believe that my walking stick is stolen property. I've been trying to tell him that I've had it for years but he won't accept my story. I believe he's been unsuccessful in reaching Detective Butler, yet he isn't going to let me board my plane." He smiled sadly. "I believe we are on the same flight."

"We'll see about that." Blood boiling, Molly tugged on Officer Reynolds's sleeve as he finished leaving a long voicemail message for Butler. "Mr. Frazier has been using this cane since the beginning of the show. I saw it myself on both Friday and Saturday." She lowered her voice. "The *missing* cane has a snake's head. Mr. Frazier's cane has a hand holding a bird as a handle. Just look at it!"

Reynolds put his hands on his hips and put on his best authoritative look. "I can't take your word on this, ma'am. You're a civilian."

The passengers in the waiting area stirred as the gate attendant announced that preboarding had begun.

"They're playing my song," Dennis said to Reynolds. "'People who need a little extra time.' That's me!" He turned to the skycap. "Ready, Harry?"

"Yessir." Harry, who closely resembled a professional linebacker, brushed Reynolds's shoulder as he moved past the young cop, bearing Dennis Frazier's carry-on.

"You have no right to detain him," Molly hurriedly whispered to Reynolds. "Butler let him go or he wouldn't be here right now. Just look at the poor man."

Reynolds watched Frazier hobble toward the gate attendant, his boarding pass crumpled in the hand that bore down on his walking stick as his splinted hand curled uselessly at his side. "Yeah, guess he doesn't quite fit the profile. I'd better get back to the hotel. There's still some dealers we've gotta give the thumbs-up to before they can roll on out. Have a good flight." He smiled and walked off.

By the time Molly and Clara boarded, Dennis was already seated in first class. As she walked by, Molly tried to catch the folk art dealer's eye, but he was staring out the window, his face as dark as the heavy sky. Molly longed to say something kind to him, but decided that it was best to let the troubled man alone.

As if watching Dennis's humiliation weren't enough to sour Molly's mood, the presence of the passenger who would be sitting to her right for the duration of the flight made her want to cry. It was Al, insurance salesman and nightmare extraordinaire to women in airplanes across the nation.

The plane had barely touched ground when Molly had unbuckled her seat belt and prepared to flee the confines of the claustrophobic space. After bearing the agony of listening to every last detail of Al's fun-filled and lucrative weekend in combination with his fetid breath and the pounds of flesh that continuously invaded the area below their shared armrest for two hours, Molly was ready to use the emergency exit over the wing to get away. Unfortunately for her, runway traffic at the Raleigh-Durham airport was heavily backed up due to the rain, which fell in violent sheets and made the black runways look slick as polished onyx. They sat on the tarmac for thirty minutes and then finally began a slow crawl to the gate.

"Hallelujah, I'm free at last!" Molly sang as she and Clara escaped the stale air inside the airplane in exchange for the tantalizing smell of fresh coffee and cinnamon buns at a café near their gate. The rain continued to pour down outside the terminal windows and another batch of glum passengers paced restlessly around the waiting area.

Clara stopped at the first restroom she saw. "Sorry, but the sound of that rain plus all of that coffee on the plane . . . be back in a bit." But just as she was about to enter the ladies' room, a maintenance worker placed a sign reading CLOSED FOR SERVICE across the entrance.

"Oh, bother!" Clara scowled.

"You can use the one down at baggage claim." The worker smiled helpfully. "It's just been cleaned."

At least three dozen women were in line to use the bathroom by the baggage claim. "Can't you wait until you get home?" Molly asked, longing to put an official end to the trip by sprawling out on her comfy couch with a throw blanket, a bag of Doritos, and her two cats purring contentedly beside her.

"No, I can't!" Clara snapped, her patience worn thin by the seemingly endless plane ride. "We don't all have the bladders of a camel, you know. Giving birth to *you* was what weakened mine." She stomped off toward the end of the line of fidgety women.

Molly wheeled her carry-on over to baggage claim in order to wait for her physician's cane and game board, both of which had been expertly packaged at the hotel for what proved to be a very bumpy ride from Nashville to Raleigh-Durham. After retrieving both boxes, Molly settled herself onto a cushioned bench facing the exit doors and watched as stressed and weary travelers prepared to make the final leg of their journeys home.

As she observed people sprinting through the rain in order to reach taxis or the dry interiors of a family member's car, she saw a dark gray town car glide through the rain like a shark swimming in the depths of the sea. The driver, wearing a professional black driver's cap and black gloves, pulled up to within inches of the bumper belonging to the minivan in front of him, dashed out of the car, and opened an enormous black umbrella using such smooth, fluid movements that Molly doubted whether a single raindrop had managed to land on his wool cap.

The driver popped open the trunk and began to load two suitcases inside with the help of one of the airport's baggage porters. The driver then opened the rear passenger door and held the umbrella over the head of his passenger so that his own was no longer protected. Limping carefully to the car, Dennis Frazier paused to hand the porter a bill. The tip must have been generous as Molly could see the drenched porter mouth an exuberant *Thank you* from where she sat just inside the door.

After Dennis was settled in his seat, he twisted his torso and reached his good arm across his body in order to accept a package from the porter. Jumping to assist, the driver and the porter grabbed a long and narrow cardboard box at the same time. The box was clearly saturated and the jarring motion made by the two strong men caused it to split open at the end closest to Dennis. Its contents, pressed forward due to the downward angle with which the porter now held the box, began to slide out on a collision course with a stream of brown water that rushed alongside the edge of the curb.

As Molly stared, her lungs stuffed with unreleased breath, she saw Dennis's right hand—his splinted and crippled hand—shoot out from the helpless position in which it normally rested in order to grab the bubble-wrapped object. Saved from the water, the object was pulled into the interior of the car as the porter and the driver shouted at one another. Neither man had seen Dennis use his damaged hand. Stunned, Molly looked down at her cardboard box. The shape of her own bubble-wrapped object was similar to Dennis's. Something thin and about three feet long. A walking stick.

Tom's words to Cotton suddenly surged through her mind. *Now I know how he got away with it,* Tom had told his friend.

Eerily, Dennis paused a moment before shutting his door. As if he sensed he was being watched, he looked directly at where Molly sat in frozen shock, the rest of the world moving busily around her. They stared at one another for what seemed like a long time. The only sounds that registered in Molly's mind were the relentless rain and the drumming of distant thunder.

And then Dennis Frazier, eyes smiling as if sharing a secret with a friend, put his hands to his lips and mouthed, *Shhhhh*. The town car eased into traffic and disappeared around a bend.

"Can't you wait until we get home to use the phone?" Clara complained when she had returned from the restroom. She put one hand on her hip and tapped her foot impatiently. "I thought you were in such a hurry."

"Detective Butler?" Molly spoke into her phone. "Dennis Frazier is the killer. What?" She blinked in surprise, her face pinched and ashen. "Yeah, I'll hold."

Chapter 14

"The long empty hours which make up a prisoner's life have always enticed inmates of jails, prisons or concentration camps to do something with their hands. A large collection can be made up exclusively of canes made by prisoners of war from a multitude of campaigns."

CATHERINE DIKE, CANES IN THE UNITED STATES

Hours later, Molly was sitting in her tiny living room, a steaming cup of lemon tea set on top of the vintage storage crate she used as a coffee table. Her cats, Merlin and Griffin, were recently fed and had been given a mountain of treats by way of apology for their mother's three-day absence. Merlin had quickly forgiven her and was nestled against her thigh, exuding warmth as he slept. Griffin, her persnickety tabby, was still giving her the cold shoulder. He had retreated to one of his favorite perches, the top of her mammoth arts and crafts bookcase. From his vantage point, at which his restless tail practically brushed the ceiling, he was able to watch Molly repeat what she had seen at the airport to Detective Jane McDowell of the Raleigh Police Department.

Detective McDowell was an attractive woman in her late thirties with shiny blond hair and vibrant blue eyes. She had a runner's body and wore very little makeup. She had appeared on Molly's doorstep within twenty minutes of Molly's return from dropping Clara off at her house in Hillsborough, knocking purposefully and refusing any refreshment.

"Detective Butler and I have been on the phone all morning," she informed Molly after listening to her story. "He wanted details on the Juliette Frazier murder four years ago. That was my case. My *first* case as a lead detective." She frowned. "We never found the murder weapon and had no solid evidence against the husband. All of a sudden, four years later, someone gets attacked in Nashville and ends up with the same kind of puncture wound to the throat. Only difference is, Mrs. Frazier wasn't lucky enough to be wearing a neck brace. She died minutes after being stabbed."

"I don't get it," Molly admitted. "Juliette and Cotton were stabbed by the same weapon?"

"Butler and I figure that the stolen snake cane is actually the murder weapon from the Frazier case." Merlin jumped down from the sofa and leapt into McDowell's lap. The pretty detective began stroking his black fur until rumbling purrs filled the room. "Of course, we've got no proof unless we can get our hands on Dennis Frazier or that cane."

"So you think that he's been faking a handicap for four years?" Molly asked, astounded by the possibility.

"Yes, I do!" McDowell exclaimed with fervor. "All along, I felt there was something wrong about Dennis. I looked up the accident report that caused his hand injury. His claim was that he had driven his car into a tree in order to avoid a deer. The leg injury was an old one—a motorcycle accident in college, but the hand injury supposedly occurred during that car accident two weeks prior to his wife's death." She sighed. "He had medical reports showing crushed bones in his wrist, a decent alibi—he had been doing some research at a local bookstore and several employees remember seeing him there—and he appeared remorseful. The case would never have made it to court, so we cut him loose."

"Still, you thought he killed her."

McDowell nodded. "Things were just lined up so nice and tidy for him. And when he talked about his wife, he was too neutral. He admitted that their relationship had been strained lately, but that he had loved Juliette deeply. I knew that was a lie by looking into his eyes. And if he told one lie, he was probably telling others."

Merlin stretched out and yawned and then began to bathe the detective's hand with his scratchy, pink tongue. "Frazier claimed that a walking stick was taken from his home the night of the murder. He said it wasn't worth more than a thousand bucks, but he believed Juliette's killer must have stolen the stick. When Butler called me and mentioned the snake cane, I knew it was the same one missing from the Frazier home."

"I guess Dennis really wanted it back."

McDowell gazed at the rain outside Molly's front window. It hadn't abated in the slightest over the last hour. "This is what Butler and I figure: Somehow this poor Tom Barnett fellow got a hold of the cane. He bought it from a small auction company in Mebane two years ago. When it didn't sell from his shop he brought it to this antique show to sell. Frazier saw the stick and decided to steal it. We figure Barnett witnessed this and maybe saw Dennis use his bad hand, so Tom was a threat and needed to be eliminated. Then Frazier tried to get Tom's inventory book from Cotton's room so that he would possess the only current record about the snake cane. Unfortunately, Cotton came back to his room too soon and Frazier attacked him using some kind of stiletto-type blade hidden inside the cane."

"That doesn't make sense," Molly argued. "How would Dennis have known that Cotton had the inventory book in the first place?"

"We don't have all the answers yet, but I know now that my instincts about that man were dead on. He's a killer, twice over." She closed her notebook. "Our challenge now is to find him."

Molly's hand shook violently as she was about to sip her tea. The hot, brown liquid slopped over the rim and onto her hand, scalding the skin of her wrist. "Ow!" She put her cup back down and sucked on her sore flesh. "What do you mean 'find him'? I called from the airport! How far could he have gotten?"

"Well, in the first place, he never went home," McDowell said. "He's a crafty guy and I'm sure he's had an escape plan in place since he killed his wife. We'll get him, but in the meantime, you're an important eyewitness." She rubbed Merlin behind the ears. "I'll be frank with you, Ms. Appleby. You may also be in danger. I think Frazier will run, but there's a slight chance that he will try to come after you."

"What should I do?" Molly felt her heart pounding in time with the rain.

"Stay someplace else, for starters. You need to pack a bag and leave right now, while I'm still here. I'm going to make sure no one's tailing you." She handed Molly her card. "I wish I could offer to do more, but we don't officially have a case yet, only suspicions."

"Can I stay with my mother?"

McDowell shook her head. "Too risky. Butler told me that she's in the antique business, too. Frazier could easily find her. We've already spoken with her, in fact. She says she's going to stay with the Lewises and that you're to go to . . ." She consulted her notebook. "A Mark Harrison's apartment. Apparently, he's at home waiting for you."

"Oh, he is, is he?" Molly felt anger swelling inside her. "I just got here. I want to stay home!" she complained, venting her frustration on one of her couch pillows. Feeling completely juvenile, she reached out and snatched Merlin from the detective's lap. "All I want to do is eat a big plate of spaghetti and sleep in my own bed tonight," she whined, nuzzling the squirming feline.

McDowell was unmoved by the temperamental display. "How does five minutes sound? We'll leave then."

"I've missed you so much!" Mark pronounced and wrapped his arms around Molly. She remained standing stiffly on his doorstep and made no move to return the embrace. Unperturbed, Mark took her suitcase and brought it inside his loft apartment. "I've ordered takeout from Sushi Yoshi. Salad with ginger dressing, dumplings, chicken teriyaki, and rice. And I've got java chip ice cream for dessert. I figured you'd need some comfort food." He put her suitcase down in the living room, went into the kitchen, and poured two glasses of ice water. "This place is a fortress, you know." He gestured at the brick walls and the double-paned windows. "Security door, peepholes, my nosy neighbor who reports everyone from the Domino's guy to my other neighbor's latest boyfriends to the super. I'm also going to drive you to work," he babbled on most uncharacteristically. "Every single day, until things are safe again." Mark chucked her gently on the chin. "Lady, I'm sticking to you like a piece of gum."

"How can you do that?" Molly finally found her voice. "Aren't you supposed to start your residency?" she asked crossly.

Mark sat down on one of the stools facing his kitchen counter. "If keeping you safe means not becoming a doctor right now, then so be it."

Molly looked down at her water glass and began tracing the ring of moisture it left on the counter with her index finger. She said nothing, punishing Mark with her silence.

"Look," he said gently. "I know you're mad at me and you have every right to be. I should have included you in my decision because my decision was really influenced by you."

"Oh? How do you figure?" Molly asked sharply.

"There was a clear limit to how far I could go working as a marketing director for *Collector's Weekly*. The income was fine for a bachelor, but it's not the kind of salary I'd need to be making as say, a husband, or . . . a father." Mark covered her hand with his. Despite herself, Molly began to thaw as she saw the sincerity in his blue eyes. "You know I love you, Molly Appleby."

Unwanted tears appeared in Molly's eyes. "I know. I'm sorry I yelled at you. It's just that . . . I got scared. Without seeing you at work, I'll be with you so much less. With all of my traveling, it's been hard enough to find time to be together."

Mark squeezed her fingers. "It's going to get even harder. The hours I'm going to be spending at the hospital and at the library doing research . . . Molly, it's going to be a real test of our relationship."

"Great." she sighed. "*That's* something to look forward to. First, I can be stalked by a murderer and then I can spend the next year watching *Sex in the City* reruns while eating frozen dinners with my cats."

"It's only for a year," Mark said soothingly. "Then I figure," he drank a gulp of water as if his throat suddenly had grown dry, "we should get married."

Molly's face lit up with a radiant smile. "Most people get engaged first, you know."

"I know." He kissed her. "But some things have to be left a surprise. I've got my plans, but they're a secret."

Just as Molly put her arms around Mark, her mind swimming with visions of a Christmas engagement, the buzzer by his apartment door sounded. "That'll be our dinner. You stay here," Mark warned. He picked up his wallet and a baseball bat and went out into the hall to meet the deliveryman at the outer door. Molly sat at the counter, staring at her empty ring finger and grinning like a fool.

* * *

A week later Molly was still trying to get used to Mark's empty office at work. He dropped her off each day as promised, hours earlier than she wanted, and then Clayton would deliver her to the library at Duke University, where she would wait until long after dinner for Mark to arrive. The arrangement had its ups and downs. On one hand, Molly had gotten a great deal of writing accomplished— three lengthy articles about Heart of Dixie and a colorful piece on the tailgate show. The e-mails had already begun pouring in as a response to her memorial piece on Tom Barnett, and the cover story on his mysterious death combined with Cotton's stabbing had the phones ringing off the hook. Ad sales had doubled for the following month and Swanson had even bought pizza for all the employees on Wednesday. Despite these successes, Molly was growing tired of living such a restricted schedule. After all, eating takeout at nine or ten every night was well past her customary dinner hour and her plans for beginning a diet had completely evaporated.

"I'm worried about my cats," Molly confided to Clayton as he handed her an iced chai tea.

"I don't know *how* you can allow that stuff to pass your lips," he grimaced. "Coconut milk? Ew!" Clayton examined the thick layer of foam on his vanilla soy latté. "Perfection."

"You should talk, Mr. Soy. Ew!" Molly mocked her friend. "Anyway, I was talking about my cats. . . ."

"Oh please, your little furballs will be fine. And speaking of fur, did you get a load of our new marketing director? I've seen chimps with less back hair. I mean, it was creeping out of his shirt like the weeds growing in my vegetable garden." Clayton inspected his manicured nails. "I was hoping for someone more like Mark and less like Swineson. Instead, we get an extra from *Planet of the*

Apes. Why, the man can't even speak except in monosyllables. How is he going to *sell* anything. Sales takes pizzazz and charisma, not grunts!"

Molly laughed. "And what is the primate's name?"

"Hairy, with an *i*." Clayton giggled. "Actually, it's Troy something or other."

Slurping the dregs of her tea, Molly could feel the sugary concoction coursing through her system. "Speaking of new men in our lives, how is the divine young man you met at the wine bar last weekend? I've been so self-absorbed I forgot to ask. Sorry."

Clayton beamed, displayed a perfect row of stark-white choppers. "Jayson with a *y* is simply delicious! We are having *such* fun! The only thing is, he's been acting so weird the last few days. He *says* it's not anything I did—as *if*— and that it's a work problem. But darling, how traumatizing can it be to work for a folk art dealer? *He* doesn't have to deal with the likes of Swanson! His boss isn't even there half the—"

"Clayton!" Molly roughly seized his arm. "Didn't you say that Jayson works for a folk art dealer in Chapel Hill?"

"Yes! Now let go of the silk, you little minx." He frowned as he scrutinized his shirt, which was the color of buttercups. "Oh, a wrinkle! I'll have to change my *whole* outfit now before I meet Jayson for dinner at 411 West."

Molly grabbed his soft hands instead. "Listen to me, Clayton. What are the chances that Jayson is actually *Dennis Frazer's assistant*? That would explain his work problems!"

"Sweet Jesus in heaven!" Clayton shrieked, stood up, and then plunked back down into his seat, covering his mouth with his fingertips "Why wouldn't he have told me?"

"Because he probably thinks his boss is innocent. *I* certainly did! The man is an incredible actor and I'm sure Jayson feels very loyal to him."

Clayton calmed down slightly. "Well, he *is* a sensitive boy." He gazed appreciatively at his own reflection in the café's wall-length mirror. "And I hope he's loyal. Oh, Miss Molly, do you think Jayson knows where Dennis is hiding?"

"He might, Clayton." Molly looked deep into his eyes. "You may be the key to my freedom! You might also be the one person who can see that justice is done for both Tom and Cotton."

"Don't forget Juliette Frazier—even though she was a *terrible* snob." Clayton's eyes shone. "Leave it to me, darling. James Bond could learn a thing or two from yours truly!" He preened happily. "Let's go. I've got to deliver you into the hands of your hunky future doctor so I can go home and primp. I'm going to have to bust out some *serious* couture for *this* mission!"

Mark was still awake at one-thirty in the morning; an enormous tome spread open before him beneath the weak light cast by a single desk lamp. Molly tossed and turned in the loft above him, waking every hour or so to wonder what had transpired between Clayton and Jayson. When the phone rang, it sounded overly loud in the late-night stillness. Molly leapt out of bed and stumbled down the dark stairs.

"Actually, she *is* awake," she heard Mark tell the caller. He held the cordless phone out to her. "It's Clayton," he said, covering the mouthpiece with his hand. "He sounds upset."

"Clayton?" she whispered, both excited and concerned.

"Honey, I think I'm single again," Clayton stated lugubriously.

"Uh-oh. What happened?"

"Well, we started our evening off drinking Cosmos at my place. Then I ordered a ridiculously expensive but sublimely smooth pinot noir to accompany our entrées at 411, followed by Irish coffee. Over chocolate mousse, Jayson was finally drunk enough to admit that his boss was Dennis Frazier, but after that, he clammed up tighter than Swanson's wallet on payday."

Molly was disappointed. "That's all you found out?"

"Hold your horses, sweetie. It is almost two in the morning and I'm already feeling a *nasty hang*over coming on!" Clayton paused, knowing that Molly was clinging to his every word. "Anyway, I started telling Jayson that the police were concerned for your safety and that as a dear friend of mine, I was *naturally* frantic with worry! He told me that Dennis would *never* hurt anyone and that the police must be wrong."

"I knew he'd think that! Dennis had everyone in the antique world convinced and they're all experts at recognizing fakes, so Jayson didn't stand a chance."

Clayton snorted. "He didn't stand a chance keeping secrets from yours truly, that's for sure! I told that poor boy that you were having *horrible* nightmares and felt you were being watched every second. I told him that I was *terribly* concerned over your mental state, and that if Dennis was stalking you, I would never forgive Jayson for protecting his boss."

"You're a real gem, do you know that?" Molly felt a rush of gratitude toward her friend.

"I haven't gotten to the best part, sugar. When I tell you this"—he waited for an infuriatingly long moment before continuing again—"you'll insist that I'm more priceless than the crown jewels!"

"Go on then!" she exclaimed and Mark shot her an irritated glance. He obviously hadn't been able to read a sentence since Clayton called.

"So I went on and on about Dennis stalking you and *finally*, Jayson blurted out, 'He's hundreds of miles away from here, so he couldn't possibly be stalking your friend!'"

Molly released her pent-up breath. "Where is he?" She was so busy imagining her next article, in which she starred as the mastermind behind Dennis Frazier's arrest, that she barely heard Clayton's answer. "Sorry, I missed that last part."

"I *said* that our date was over at that point. Jayson stormed off in a huff and I doubt he'll ever speak to me again." Clayton sniffed. "I'll leave it to you to contact the police. I break out in hives anytime I come in contact with that much polyester."

"You did the right thing, Clayton," Molly assured her friend. "Now, give me Jayson's address and phone number. I'm going to call Detective McDowell before *he* has a chance to get away."

"He was holed up in a cabin in Boone," McDowell informed Molly over coffee two days later. "A real primitive place he would lend out to some of his folk artist friends when they faced tough times. The local boys did a stakeout until we could get out there." Her eyes shone with the memory of the arrest. "Frazier never suspected we were onto him. He came out meek as a lamb. Had the snake cane with him, too. Our weapons specialist is having it X-rayed as we speak."

"Man, he was really attached to that thing," Molly said in wonder.

McDowell stirred a packet of sugar into her black coffee. "I don't normally update civilians during ongoing investigations like this, but you've earned the right to know that we're holding Frazier in Raleigh while we work something out with the boys in Nashville." She smiled. "Bottom line is, you can go home now."

Molly nodded but didn't reply. It had been a hard week living by Mark's schedule, but once she returned home she would see him even less. Today was Saturday. Normally, this was the one night of the week Molly and Mark set aside to go on a date. They usually went to dinner and a movie, but Mark had informed her earlier that day that he would be on rounds and they'd have to postpone their date indefinitely.

"You must miss those adorable cats of yours," McDowell said, sensing that Molly's mind was wandering.

Feeling a twinge of guilt, Molly said, "I do! I've got six cans of tuna fish and a package of sliced chicken breast in the car to bribe them with."

McDowell rose and gave Molly a hearty handshake. "Thanks again for your help. I'm going to sleep a whole lot better knowing that I've got a chance to correct the mistake I made four years ago." Her eyes twinkled. "I haven't made another one since." She began to walk away.

"Detective?" Molly called after her. "Do you think I could see a copy of that X-ray?"

McDowell paused. "Why?"

"It would make a great graphic for my 'Murder at Heart of Dixie' article."

"Sorry. You'll have to wait until after the case is closed." McDowell shrugged. "I can't let anything interfere with seeing Dennis Frazier brought to justice." She hesitated. "But if we can conclude that the cane is the murder weapon, I'm willing to tell you how it operated. Off the record, of course."

"Of course," Molly agreed.

Several weeks later, as Molly was watching the eleven o'clock news and waiting for Mark to call, an anchor-woman began her broadcast by flatly reporting that Dennis Frazier had confessed to first-degree murder in the state of North Carolina.

"Once the police obtained evidence that the medical records regarding Dennis Frazier's hand injury had been falsified," the anchorwoman reported, "the Chapel Hill folk art dealer confessed to killing his wife. He had badly bruised his wrist during the car accident, but it had healed sufficiently by the night of his wife's murder and he was easily able to operate the unique cane weapon that ended Juliette Frazier's life."

The camera switched to video feed of Dennis Frazier exiting a courthouse in Raleigh. The anchorwoman continued speaking. "When questioned about his motive, Frazier chillingly replied, 'Juliette was a nasty bitch who hated everything I loved. She constantly damaged my most priceless items or sold them behind my back. I could have divorced her, but something made me want to hurt her using one of my precious pieces of folk art, which she despised so much. So I chose the cane. It felt right in my hand when I held it and thought about how wonderful it would be to live alone again.' "

The camera returned its focus to the anchorwoman. "The killer cane, as the weapon has been dubbed, is also responsible for wounding an antiques dealer in Nashville on October sixteenth. The cane had been missing since the Frazier murder four years ago. How did it resurface? Courtroom reporter Tina Jennings asked Dennis Frazier that very question."

The camera returned to the same clip of Dennis on the courthouse steps. "I stored the cane in my gallery after my wife's death, but my assistant at the time sold it by mistake while I was out of town. I've been searching for it ever since. Tom Barnett had it for sale in his booth and he saw me releasing the blade before the preview party." Frazier's face crumpled before the camera. "I'm sorry about Tom. He was a good man, but I had to have that cane back."

The anchorwoman went on to speculate on the subject of whether Dennis was mentally imbalanced, but those in the antiques business had their own take on the matter.

"I'd kill *my* wife if she ever sold my collection of toy soldiers," Molly heard one dealer say to another as she attended Lex's weekly auction.

"And my husband wouldn't last a second if he deliberately broke any of my Meissen figurines. Believe me, he'd like to, but he wouldn't dare," a lady in the crowd said heatedly.

More people piped up in defense of Dennis's actions, until an elderly lady rapped on the floor with her metal cane. "Y'all are plum forgettin' about Tom Barnett! *He* didn't deserve to die! Why, half of my house is filled with treasures I bought from that dear boy. Now hush up, before I use *this* cane as a weapon."

Molly grinned at the lady, who issued her a saucy wink in return. As the auction came to a close, she said goodbye to her friend Kitty, Lex, and to her mother, and headed back to the office to type up notes about the sale.

As she plodded through the congestion on Interstate 40, which seemed as though it had been under construction for the past ten years, her mind wandered back to the photographs Detective McDowell had e-mailed her. They were of Dennis's snake cane. One was a close-up of the snake's head, showing its intricately carved scales, the bared fangs, and the haunting white eyes. The second showed the thin, sharp blade poking out through the top of the cobra's head—a blade that had claimed the lives of two people and had temporarily maimed a third.

"For your eyes only. Do not print!" McDowell had written in the e-mail, but the photos had enabled Molly to put the finishing touches on her article on Dennis Frazier and the Heart of Dixie murder.

She felt as though it was her finest piece of journalism, but so far Swanson had yet to comment on it at all, though he ran it on the cover and included a special insert containing photographs Molly had taken at the show, of Dennis's gallery in Chapel Hill, and of the Raleigh home he had once shared with Juliette.

Growing cross as she reflected on her boss's lack of enthusiasm for her work, Molly wondered if she should start looking for another job. Surely there were plenty of papers that would like to have someone with her talents on their staff. With Mark no longer working for *Collector's Weekly*, maybe she should pursue finding a job with more appreciation and better pay. Still, she frowned as she entered the familiar office building. She loved writing about antiques, and the major rival antiques and collectibles paper was located in the Northeast and she certainly didn't want to move.

Molly was so wrapped up in her thoughts that she nearly walked right by her cubicle in order to get herself a cup of coffee. The sight of Mark turning circles in her swivel chair caused her to come to an abrupt halt.

"Hello, beautiful!" He jumped up and kissed her on the cheek.

"I thought you had to work!" she said, pleased. "What are you doing here?"

"I'm going to have to go back, but I couldn't miss the celebration."

Molly looked around. There wasn't another soul in sight. "Celebration?"

"This way, milady," Mark beckoned and led her down the hall in the direction of Swanson's office.

But Carl wasn't in his office and Mark propelled her beyond Swanson's door to one of the large corner offices down the hall. The door stood open and it was dark inside, but as Molly approached the threshold, the lights suddenly came on and several people yelled, "Surprise!"

"What's going on?" Molly asked when she could speak again.

Clayton came forward carrying a paper plate bearing a cupcake. "Let the head honcho tell you himself."

All eyes turned to Swanson, who was leaning against a sleek metal desk in the otherwise stark office. He stood up, his face its usual mask of grumpiness, and cleared his throat. "You've done good work, Molly," he grunted and then stepped aside.

Molly's eyes rounded with delight as she read the desk plaque, which had been hidden behind Swanson's ample rump.

It read, *Molly Appleby, Senior Staff Writer.*

Her colleagues in her new office erupted in cheers.

Officer Pittman unlocked the door to the enormous storage space called the evidence locker by the Nashville P.D. and compared the number written on the index card with those posted on the ends of the tall metal shelves. Scowling, he moved deeper into the room, which seemed uninviting and cold with its gray cement floor and weak fluorescent track lighting. Housing thousands of implements used for the sole purpose of inflicting misery, pain, and even death, most of the officers of the police department felt an inexplicable sense of negativity within the locker, but not Officer Pittman. He experienced a surge of exhilaration as soon as he entered.

"I'm no goddamn errand boy," the young man grumbled, striking out at one of the shelves with a flat palm, enjoying how the assorted items suffocating within their clear plastic bags tottered back and forth. Pausing to investigate a folded towel spotted with what appeared to be dried blood, Pittman perked up. "Hey, maybe I got lucky getting

sent down here. This place is loaded with cool crap." He
fingered a small bag containing a thick gold chain and a
diamond-encrusted pendant shaped like a dollar sign.
"Gang bullshit," Pittman said dismissively, and then his
eye was drawn by the gleam of metal.

"Hell-o, my pretty." Pittman picked up a bag containing
a serrated boot knife. Alongside the boot knife was another
bag holding a trio of butterfly knives, blades neatly tucked
away out of sight. Pitman couldn't help but wonder if there
was any blood on the hidden blades.

Pittman loved knives. He collected them, and he had
even converted the spare room in his two-bedroom apartment into a display space for his treasures. The longest
wall was covered with an incredible variety of knives, and
the young cop had artfully arranged them into a arc, so
when the lights were turned on, the wall glimmered and
shone like some kind of deadly rainbow. He smiled just
thinking of his precious Civil War bayonets, German daggers from World War II, the large grouping of Swiss Army
knives, vintage Chinese throwing knives, aggressive-
looking machetes, Bowie knives, switchblades, and hunting
knives in worn leather cases.

Visualizing his knife room, Pittman was also reminded
that he needed to stop at the pet store on the way home to
pick up more rats or even a baby rabbit for the Boston
Strangler, his red-tailed boa. In addition to B.S., as Pittman
lovingly referred to his forty-pound pet, he might buy a
small garter snake as a special treat for Magnus, his beautiful king snake. Magnus was Pittman's special favorite
and he often took the reptile out of his tank so that the
red-, black-, and yellow-banded constrictor would wrap
himself around Pittman's shoulders as the unusual young
man watched TV.

Pittman had forgotten all about his task. He was told to
collect a kitchen chopping knife that had been used in a fatal stabbing more than ten years ago. The knife was believed

to also be the weapon used on a decomposed body recently uncovered in the wooded area of one of the county parks. Pittman meandered down the rows of silent evidence and thought about his job. He was excited to be involved in a real case of murder, even if the victim had been dead for half as long as Pittman had been alive. Up to this point in his new career he had only been appointed menial and insulting jobs like dealing with car wrecks or responding to domestic violence complaints, which usually turned out to be a couple of drunks screaming at each other in the parking lot of their apartment building. Boring stuff. A bunch of idiot civilians. Pittman wanted to draw his gun, use his club on some deserving lowlife. Why else would he have become a cop?

Pittman looked at his watch and paused, as always, to admire the rattlesnake tattoo poised to strike from the hairy flesh of his muscular forearm. It was almost lunchtime. Heading down the row that matched the numbers on his card, Pittman came to an abrupt halt before a long, slim object with a carved cobra's head. A vague memory tickled Pittman's brain.

"No way. It's the Killer Cane!" Pittman breathed reverently as he gently removed the cane from the shelf and cradled it in his arms. "I 'member you from the paper." Looking around, Pittman paused and then removed the cane from its taped bag using the small folding knife he carried at all times.

Releasing the snake cane from its plastic prison, Pittman traced the fangs with his finger and felt an overwhelming desire to possess the famous antique. He stared into the cobra's sightless white eyes and hesitated, filled with indecision. The snake seemed to whisper to him: Take me, take me. Pittman stared at it in awe, recalling exactly how the weapon cane operated from the detailed description and large photographs published in the Tennessean after Dennis Frazier's murder trial. After some searching, he located the release buttons and jumped in startled delight as the thin and lethal blade burst from within the cavity of wood.

Without further thought, Pittman rewrapped the cane, grabbed the kitchen knife he had been sent for, and headed back to the hallway. Desperate to avoid being caught stealing evidence, he stashed the cane behind a grouping of mops and brooms in the nearest maintenance closet. He would return for the weapon cane later and hide it inside his trench coat until it was safe to take it to his car. He would risk his job and much, much more to add the weapon to his collection. Such an amazing piece was not meant to sit on a cold, metal shelf. It was meant to be admired by someone who understood its beauty. Pittman already longed to release the blade again, to run his hands over the wooden scales and touch the menacing fangs.

Shaking off the feeling of longing, Pittman closed the snake into the dark closet. As he eased the door shut, a bar of light from the hallway found the snake's head and ignited its white eyes. For an insane instant, Pittman could have sworn the cobra winked at him.

A Brief Note on Gadget Canes

Canes and walking sticks have been around since the beginning of man's history, and they are as varied in form and usage as the woods from which they were made. The staff was used by shepherds before it gradually became of symbol of authority. Hundreds of years ago the staff appeared in the Bible and represented might, especially in Aaron's triumph over Pharaoh's magicians. In ancient art, staffs, and crooks were painted or sculpted into the hands of gods of ancient Egypt and Greece. Eventually, this sign of strength and power was adopted by human rulers, such as kings and emperors, and also by high-ranking members of the priesthood. Important individuals of the armed forces and of the legal system (such as judges) carried batons or staffs as symbols of their clout as well.

For centuries, the cane was restricted to its role as shepherder, crutch, or staff of authority, but during the latter part of the sixteenth century and well into the seventeenth, walking sticks were carried by the nobility as a sign of wealth and prestige. Canes and sticks became a fashion accessory that no self-respecting gentleman would do without. During this period, walking sticks became more and more decorative and were custom made according to an individual's wishes. Jewels, ivory, gold knobs, porcelain figures in recline, monogrammed initials in sterling silver, or even a carving of the owner's beloved bulldog distinguished one stick from another.

Unhappily for the upper class, the rise of the middle class in the nineteenth century allowed a much larger portion of the general populace to purchase canes. Suddenly, canes started to live a double life. Gadget canes (also called system sticks) became handy vessels in which to hold practical items, the tools of one's trade, or weapons.

The weapon cane fabricated for *A Deadly Dealer* is an example of a flick stick. This was a long, thin blade hidden in the shaft of the cane. If the owner felt as if a suspicious person were getting a little too close, the blade could be released with a sharp flick of the wrist. In addition to these thin blades, full-sized daggers and swords were also disguised within what were usually unadorned shafts with simple knobs or handles. Guns were also built into handles and the upper portion of the shaft.

However, weapon canes weren't always of such a complex nature. Instead of stabbing or shooting someone, you could beat an enemy using a blackjack cane. To use this cane, you'd pull off the handle, revealing a piece of rubber or steel that would act as a kind of flexible whip. For those who didn't have the time to draw a handle, such as the policemen of days gone by, a stick with a weighted knob would do. These sticks had round, heavy knobs created using such materials as leather-wrapped wood, brass, or a hurtful hunk of metal, such as iron. One bang on the head with one of these sticks and an adversary would be down for the count.

Gadget canes were a handy place to hide an assortment

of private things. If a person were bent on murder, a weapon cane wouldn't even be necessary. Several gadget canes could be used to transport poison. For example, many physician canes had storage spaces for small vials. It would have been perfectly plausible for a cane to bear a vial of laudanum or opium. Other liquids could be transported inside canes as well: A gentleman's cane might hold a narrow glass flask for whiskey or contain a vessel with which to siphon wine right from its wooden cask. Some of these canes also included miniature cups the size of shot glasses for instant gratification.

For those interested in amusement rather than foul play, purely recreational canes were designed to store dice, dominoes, lighters, and snuff, or to serve as golf clubs, nutcrackers, pipes, corkscrews, fishing poles, telescopes, and opera glasses—perhaps to take a closer look at the attractive members of the fairer sex seated in the audience. Women adapted the practice of wearing canes as well, although theirs had fewer purposes than those created for the men. Women's canes, though more adorned in general, were restricted to more conventional uses such as receptacles for perfume, smelling salts, or timepieces. They occasionally doubled as umbrellas, thus protecting the fair skin of their mistress from both sun and rain.

Professionals often carried the tools of their trade within their canes. The coffin maker and horse buyer's canes held measuring sticks, a photographer could carry a small camera inside or transform his stick into a tripod, the painter could store brushes and a jar of turpentine in his, and the musician could turn his cane into a violin at a moment's notice. And for those writers of times past, pens, ink, and pencils were easily stored in the handles of gadget canes.

Readers interested in collecting gadget canes may wonder how to discover if a cane has another identity hidden within. One of the easiest ways to tell is to give the cane a good shake. If something rattles within the hollow shaft, it may be that an object is indeed inside. Even hollow handles can contain small objects, such as coins or matches. Take a look at the area where the handle attaches to the shaft. Is there a clear division between the two sections? Can you feel any give when you try to twist the handle counterclockwise? This may indicate a recess in the shaft, but don't force the handle too far, as you may end up ruining a cane that isn't leading a double life. If you seriously suspect that you've just inherited a Toledo sword cane but can't get the handle to budge, you can always turn to an X-ray machine to confirm your hunch.

Keep in mind that gadget canes are typically plain on the outside, unlike the cobra weapon cane created for *A Deadly Dealer*. And if you discover a gadget cane that is loaded with too many items, then it may be a fake. If there are lots of goodies in such a cane, ranging from combs to syringes, try to look for objects that might have been out of place in the nineteenth century or don't match with one another. Gadget canes usually had one theme, not multiple themes, so avoid buying a cane that purportedly contains a coffin maker's stick along with a whiskey flask. That's not to say that coffin makers didn't enjoy their nips back then, but it's unlikely they would have mixed business with pleasure within the space of a single cane.

Of course, there are contemporary gadget canes, which are fun to collect simply for their usefulness. If you're a sports fanatic, a cane that transforms into a three-legged seat might be just the ticket. If I could find a cane that contained an éclair, a babysitter, and a masseuse, I'd buy it in a second! In any case, enjoy the hunt. Gadget canes are becoming more and more scarce, so if you see one that brings a smile to your face, buy it. If nothing else, they make fascinating show-and-tell items during dinner parties.

Examples of Gadget Canes

The perfect folk art stick for mystery lovers

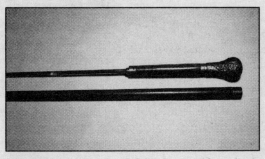

A dagger cane with a beautifully decorated brass knob

A flick stick in its closed position

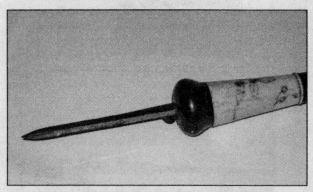

The flick stick's blade. Small but deadly.

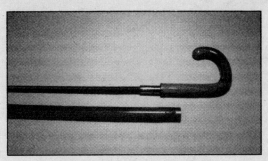

A black jack cane with a metal "whip"

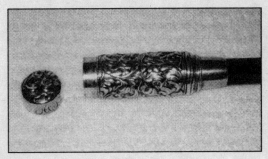

Close up of the black jack cane's handle

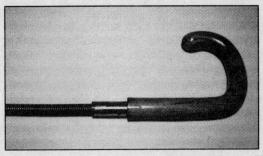

A sterling silver vinaigrette cane

Acknowledgments

I'd like to thank Holly Hudson and Pamala Briggs for testing out the manuscript; my agent, Jessica Faust; and my editor, Samantha Mandor. I'm also grateful for the medical expertise of Dr. Theodore Stanley, who filled me in on all the nuances of opium; to Brad Hamphauer of Hamphauer Canes for sharing his passion for canes and for getting me started on my collection; Leland Little for displaying the Molly Appleby books at his gallery; Jessica Pack for taking books to shows; and lastly, but most importantly, to my family—all of whom have cheered Molly and me from the get go. I love you guys.

ABOUT THE AUTHOR

A former middle school English teacher, **J. B. Stanley** has dabbled in the antiques and collectibles world by trading on eBay, working part-time at auction houses, and contributing articles for *Antiqueweek*. Having lived in central North Carolina for eight years, J. B. Stanley now resides in Richmond with her husband, two young children, and three cats. For more information, please visit www.jbstanley.com.